# WEIRD KID

Also by Greg van Eekhout

*Voyage of the Dogs*

*Cog*

# WEIRD KID

# KID

## GREG VAN EEKHOUT

HARPER

*An Imprint of HarperCollinsPublishers*

Library of Congress Cataloging-in-Publication Data

Names: van Eekhout, Greg, author.

Title: Weird kid / Greg van Eekhout.

Description: First edition. | New York, NY : Harper, an imprint of HarperCollins Publishers, 2021. | Audience: Ages 8-12. | Audience: Grades 4-6. | Summary: Jake Foster, a shapeshifting alien of goo disguised as a human, and his spunky friend Agnes investigate the mysterious takeover of their neighbors by "imblobsters" and uncover the reason Jake is losing control of his ability to keep his human shape.

Identifiers: LCCN 2020040566 | ISBN 978-0-06297060-2 (hardcover)

Subjects: CYAC: Extraterrestrial beings—Fiction. | Friendship—Fiction. | Shapeshifting—Fiction. | Humorous stories.

Classification: LCC PZ7.V2744 We 2021 | DDC [Fic]—dc23

LC record available at https://lccn.loc.gov/2020040566

Typography by Chris Kwon

22 23 24 25 26  LSB  6 5 4 3 2

First Edition

*To all the weird kids: Stay weird.*

✦ ✦ ✦

# CHAPTER 1

**TOMORROW I'LL BE AMONG PEOPLE,** so tonight I practice my smile.

Smiling should be easy. You pull up the corners of your mouth, maybe show some teeth, maybe don't, and that's it, you're smiling.

Or, if you're me, you grow a forked snake tongue, just for fun.

But only when nobody's looking.

Only when you want to.

At least, that's how it used to be.

Tomorrow's the first day of middle school, and I have to keep my mouth and body under control, or else.

I face the bathroom mirror and try a smile, bright and friendly.

My teeth are all wrong.

Too small, too many, shaped like tiny, sharp arrowheads.

"Piranha teeth, great," I mutter, being careful not to cut my tongue.

Things started going haywire in June. That's when *I* started going haywire. I was at the grocery store with Mom, helping her pick out avocados for Tuesday Taco Night, and I had to get around an old man blocking the aisle. "Excuse me, sir," I said, and he gave me a huge smile and told me I was very polite. For some reason the phrase "ear-to-ear grin" popped into my brain, and before I knew it, my mouth stretched so wide it curved around my face in an actual ear-to-ear grin. The top of my head might have toppled off if I'd smiled any bigger.

The old man screamed and ended up needing EMTs and oxygen and Mom rushed me out of the store and we didn't have guacamole with our tacos that night.

That wasn't my only accidental shapeshifting this summer. A week after the grocery store, I was bouncing on the trampoline in the backyard. On my last landing, my body flattened into a big tortilla. I managed to re-form my human shape after a few seconds, but if the neighbors had seen . . .

Shifting in public is very dangerous.

*They* could find out about me.

*They* is the police.

*They* is government agents.

*They* is my teachers and classmates. *They* is my friends.

*They* could be anyone.

That's what Mom and Dad tell me all the time.

I try another smile in the mirror, just a tiny one.

I can do this. I've smiled before, hundreds of times. I'm just having some new-school nerves. I'm just freaking myself out.

Close my eyes.

Take a breath.

Think normal thoughts.

I open my eyes. Staring back at me is a Venus flytrap.

I am doomed.


The drop-off curb in front of Cedar Creek View Middle School is a chaos of cars and slamming doors and screaming kids. Mom and Dad insisted on driving me, even though I could have walked or ridden my bike. They say delivering me to school makes things easier, but I know this is a test.

Mom turns to look back at me. "Feeling good about today?"

What she means is, "Have you accidentally grown eye-stalks? Have you reverted to pure goo form? Do you need a bucket?"

Mom and Dad wanted to start homeschooling me to prevent anyone from discovering my secret, but I refused. I want to do normal things. I want to eat stale chicken nuggets in the cafeteria. I want to hang out with my friends. I want to sketch guitars on my math worksheets instead of doing actual math.

I won the fight, so I get to go to regular school, but if I have a shifting episode they'll pull me right out.

"Any cramps?" Dad asks.

"No."

"Burning sensations?"

"No."

"Excessive itching? Strange wriggling?"

"No, Dad. No."

Dad's a proctologist. That means he's a medical doctor

who specializes in butts. Asking about symptoms is how he shows he cares.

As soon as the car stops I leap out. I'm ten steps away before they stop me.

"Jake!"

With a groan, I turn around.

Dad's holding out my lunch card.

I tromp back and pluck it from his outstretched hand.

"I love you, kid," he says.

Mom smiles. "Have a wonderful first day, Jake-o-lantern."

I wave but don't smile back because I don't want to risk my mouth doing something weird.

A few minutes of shuffling and dodging through the clogged halls gets me to my first class, Advisory. "Sit anywhere," the teacher says, not looking up from the stack of papers on his desk. Class doesn't even start for another five minutes, and he already seems stressed. I get it.

I gaze out into a sea of faces and instantly regret it, because now a sea of faces is looking back at me. What's my mouth doing? Is it normal-sized? Do I have extra rows of teeth? Do I have tusks? Nobody's screaming, so it's probably good.

Cedar Creek View Middle School takes students from all seven elementary schools in our district, so instead of a few hundred kids, now I'm going to school with almost a thousand. Only a few of the faces are familiar.

I catch sight of Eirryk near the window and give him a nod. Our eyes lock for a second before he looks away, pretending he didn't see me.

Eirryk and I are best friends. Or we used to be. Things changed over the summer. He just wanted to hang out the way we normally did, jumping our bikes off a plywood ramp in front of his house, shooting hoops, playing putt-putt golf. But I couldn't risk shifting into jelly at the water park, so I kept putting him off, making excuses. One day it'd be a dentist appointment. Then, I'd tell him I had a stomachache. Then, chicken pox. After a month of that, he gave up on me. And I can't blame him.

I duck my head and aim for a seat in the back row.

A few more kids straggle in. The final one, a tall white girl, takes the empty seat next to me. I notice her backpack, stuffed so full that the zipper doesn't shut. I also notice a purple-and-green snake poking out of it. After another second or two of looking at it, I realize it's not a snake but a coil of climbing rope, which is maybe not as weird a thing to bring to school as a snake, but it's unusual. And the third thing I notice is the patch sewn on the shoulder of her denim jacket. It's the wing logo of Night Kite, my second-favorite comic book character. Night Kite doesn't have any superpowers, but by training her mind and body she turned herself into a living weapon against evil.

My first-favorite character is Star Hammer, an alien who lives secretly among humans on Earth.

I look up from the girl's patch to find her frowning at me.

"What's wrong?" I ask, dreading the answer.

Without breaking eye contact, she jots something down in a little black notebook. "You're Jake Wind."

"How do you know—?"

The school bell chimes, and Mr. Brown tells us to be quiet.

He goes over some announcements and rules and the student conduct code. A lot of time is spent on the subject of chewing gum.

"Gum is disgusting," he rants. "I don't want to see gum stuck under your seats. I don't want to see it between your teeth. I don't want to hear it smacking in your mouth. I don't even want to see it in its wrapper."

I find gum relatable since it can be transformed from a rigid rectangle into a shapeless wad, but Mr. Brown has a zero-tolerance gum policy.

Now that Mr. Brown has expressed his feelings, he finally gets around to taking roll. I learn that the girl with the Night Kite patch is named Agnes Oakes.

My nerves get jangly when Mr. Brown gets to the *S* names, because it means he's getting to the end of the alphabet, which means he's going to call on me soon, which means at least a few kids are going to turn around to look at me when I raise my hand. My heart pounds and my fingers twitch and my face tingles and there's a big resounding hum between my ears and I wish I could just fly away like a bird.

"Jake Wind," Mr. Brown calls.

Wishing bird-related thoughts turns out to be a mistake.

I've sprouted feathers on my right hand. Actual bird feathers, speckled brown and gold.

This is a first.

"Jake Wind?"

I tuck my right hand under my desk, between my knees.

"Jake Wind, going once, going twice . . ."

"Here!" I squeak, putting my left hand up.

Mr. Brown looks at me. Kids look at me. All of them, looking at me. Please, oh, please, don't let my mouth have turned into a bird beak.

"Parker Zeballos," calls Mr. Brown, moving on.

I guess my mouth did not transform into a bird beak.

The humming in my head softens and my hand reverts to normal and I let myself breathe now that everyone's looking at Parker, a girl in the third row.

Everyone but Agnes Oakes.

She stares into my face and scribbles furiously in her notebook.

# CHAPTER 2

**I SURVIVE THREE MORE CLASSES,** most of which I spend devising a brilliant scheme to protect myself from the prying eyes of Agnes Oakes.

I, Jake Wind, will disappear.

In my place will be a completely different kid.

"Bonjour," this different kid will say. "I am Marcel. I am from France."

There are only two small flaws in my plan.

One: I can't shift into a whole other person. Forked tongues, yes. Totally shifting from one thing into a complete other thing? No way.

Two: I don't speak French.

It's a garbage plan, pretty much.

Lunch is weird and I don't know what to do with myself. At my old school, each class sat together at the same cafeteria table, but at Cedar Creek View Middle School, you can sit wherever you want, at any table, inside or outside. It's too many choices. I wander around with my recyclable cardboard tray of stale chicken nuggets and carrot sticks and nonfat milk and spot Eirryk squatting on a log next to the main office. I catch his eye and try a nod. For the second time today, he acts like he doesn't see me and turns to the rest of the kids he's sitting with. The only one of them I know is Adrian Thacker. Adrian was in swim club with me and Eirryk at the city pool for three summers in a row, but I didn't join this summer because of my shapeshifitng problems. Adrian glances at me, says something to Eirryk, and they both laugh. I can't hear what they're saying, but I'm pretty sure they're laughing at me. I don't know why. What's so funny about me?

I feel almost as weird as I did when I had a bird hand.

And as if things weren't bad enough, my bones are starting to ache from the Hum.

The Hum is a low, deep vibration I started feeling early this summer.

Right around the time I started losing control over my shifting.

I know, right?

Sometimes it lasts just a few seconds. Sometimes it's sort of in the background, like a ringing in my ears, only through my whole body. And sometimes it's really strong and I lose form and have to spend some time in a bucket.

I wish I had a bucket right now.

I find a quiet place on the edge of the soccer field and sit down to gnaw nuggets and hopefully not soak through the grass.

"Jake Wind, I know all about you."

It's Agnes Oakes, hurrying toward me like she's late for something and angry about it. "I've discovered your secret." She crosses her wrists and flaps her hands like bird wings.

A million words gargle up from my belly. Fortunately, none of them spill out, because screaming "I am not an alien shapeshifter!" is a pretty bad way to keep a secret.

"Night Kite," Agnes says, impatient. "You're a Night Kite fan." She makes flapping wings again.

"Oh! You saw me staring at your patch?" The flapping hands is Night Kite's secret signal to her allies. I check to make sure my hands are normal before returning the gesture.

Agnes nods. "My mom and I just moved to Cedar Creek View from San Diego, and your mom met my mom at the gym. They started talking and my mom said I don't have any friends because I'm new and your mom said she's afraid you'll have a hard time adjusting to middle school, so our moms decided we should be friends. Which I wasn't sure about, but since you like Night Kite, maybe it'll be okay."

"Um," I say.

"Why do they call this place Cedar Creek View, anyway? There aren't any cedar trees and there's no creek."

"Right, so no view of either. I never thought about it."

"I can't *stop* thinking about it. Can I sit?"

I scooch to make room for her, even though we have the whole soccer field to ourselves.

She munches on her own nuggets. "What's your favorite *Night Kite* issue?"

I don't even have to think about it. "I like the crossover with Star Hammer."

She gives me a nod. "The power of Star Hammer combined with the brains and skill of Night Kite. They should give the two of them their own team-up book."

"Did you like her in *Human Grenade* 273?"

She makes a face. "The art was kinda weird on that

one. What did you think about *Star Hammer* double-sized issue 50?"

That's the one where the last survivors of Star Hammer's home planet, Bahlpeen, come to take over Earth, and Star Hammer uses the Celestial Mallet to smash the Bahlpeenians into atoms, and that makes him the only Bahlpeenian in the entire universe, which I totally relate to since I'm the only one like me in Cedar Creek View and possibly the entire planet.

"The art was kinda weird on that one, too," is all I say.

Before I know it, I'm blathering about comics with Agnes Oakes like we're old friends. And feeling slightly less weird.

I almost forget about the Hum.

But only for a minute.

Because the Hum gets stronger.

My belly wriggles like it's trying to escape my body. And those butt symptoms my dad likes to ask about? I have them everywhere. My eyes itch. My scalp convulses. My skin feels like bubbling oatmeal.

Keep it together, I tell myself. You are Jake, a totally boring absolutely non-weird and completely solid individual.

I can tell myself anything, but that doesn't mean my body will listen.

A tiny squeak escapes my lips as my right thumb sprouts little miniature thumbs like branches. A thumb tree is not something I'd ever imagined, and now I've got one.

My whole world vibrates. Desperately, I shove all my thumbs in my pocket and search my head for French words in case I need to activate Marcel.

Luckily, Agnes isn't paying attention to me. I'm wriggling and weird, but so is the ground. The earth sags, and the grass we're sitting on tilts down. Clumps of turf break loose and slide like puzzle pieces off an upended table into an expanding hole.

Agnes and I scrabble backward, trying to get away from the arcade-air-hockey-sized chasm. Agnes grabs my arms to keep me from falling in, and I do the same to her with my non-thumb-tree hand.

Finally, things settle. Red soil sifts. Pebbles click-clack into the hole.

"What just happened?" I ask.

Agnes springs to her feet and leans over the edge of the hole.

"Sinkhole! Unstable ground gives way and everything above it collapses. And we were lucky enough to witness it!"

I do not feel very lucky.

Kids are running over as if there's a cool fight to see. Whistles shriek as teachers and yard supervisors try to call them back.

While Agnes peers into the darkness below, I check out my thumb-hand and touch my ears and run my tongue over my teeth. Everything seems normal on the outside. On the inside I feel like soft-serve ice cream.

"Look at that!" Agnes says, pointing into the hole. "There's some kind of ooze."

"More like goo than ooze," I say like I'm an expert on the difference between ooze and goo. Which I am, but why announce it?

The goo squirms from the ground near the rim of the hole, like an earthworm after a rain, except it's big as a breakfast sausage link. It looks familiar. Not quite cake batter. Sort of what I look like when I go liquid. Like Jake batter.

Now kids crowd around the hole, shouting, laughing, pretending to push each other in.

Agnes takes a deep breath. *"OH MY GOD THERE'S A DEAD BODY DOWN THERE!"*

Everyone gets excited, shoving each other out of the way to get a better look, even the teachers. While they're all distracted, Agnes drops to her knees, spoons the goo sausage into a plastic cup, screws the cap on, and seals it with a strip of tape.

Why is she equipped with a spoon and a cup with a lid and tape?

"My mistake," she says. "No corpse. It was probably just a trick of light."

The teachers and supervisors yell and herd us away. As we trudge off the field, lagging behind everyone else, Agnes holds her sample up, squinting.

"Sinkhole. Strange goo. You know what this means, Jake?"

Hum plus thumb tree plus sinkhole.

"Not exactly," I tell her. Which is the truth.

"Me neither. Want to help me find out?"

Do I want to encourage this person I don't know to investigate something that, in some way, has everything to do with me?

No.

But do I want to spend time with someone who's totally into Night Kite, a superhero with scary-good detective skills who suspends bad guys off bridges to get answers from them? And do I want some answers for myself?

"Yeah," I find myself saying. "Let's figure this out."

# CHAPTER 3

**AFTER SCHOOL, AGNES GETS ON** her bike to go home, the goo safely sealed inside the plastic cup, snug in her backpack. "I'll contact you when I have results from my analysis," she assures me.

She talks just the way Night Kite does. I like it. It's nice not to be the only weird kid in school.

My parents collect me at the pickup curb, and I'm not even in the car before they start peppering me with questions.

"How did your day go?"

"Did you have lunch with your friends?"

"How were the chicken nuggets?"

"Did you meet Agnes Oakes?"

"Any burning, itching, or wriggling?"

"Okay, not really, rubbery, yes, no, no, and jeez, Dad."

I tell my parents about the two boys in my math class who got in a fight because they're both named Clint and there can be only one. And I tell them about our Physical Wellness teacher who got a leg cramp while lecturing us about the importance of staying hydrated when exercising in hot Arizona desert conditions. And I tell them about the sinkhole. But not about the goo strand. Or the stomach wriggling.

Mom and Dad taught me that you can lie by saying something that's not true, and you can lie by leaving out something that *is* true. The second type of lie is called a lie of omission.

I am omitting through my teeth.

"That's the third sinkhole in town this week," Mom says.

Dad parks the car in front of Dale's Guitar Shed. "Someone's got to do something about this before anyone get hurt."

"Yes, definitely," I agree, leaving out the part where Agnes and I have a plan to be "someone."

Dad reaches for a short stack of stamped envelopes. "I

need to mail these, and then your mom and I will be working in the coffee shop across the street."

It's just bills and magazine subscriptions, boring stuff, but I jump at the opportunity.

"I'll do it!"

Dad laughs. "Yeah, I thought you might."

Whenever we're downtown and there's something to mail, I volunteer. Because of Big Blue Biter.

Big Blue Biter is the mailbox on the corner. It looks like a regular mailbox, painted blue steel with a curved top and a hinged lid, but it's not at all regular. It has a reputation.

With my guitar bag on my back and letters in hand, I approach slowly, as if it's a sleeping panther. Most people approach it this same way. Big Blue Biter's been on this corner as long as I've been alive. I don't know why I enjoy dropping letters inside. Is it the danger? The excitement? Don't ask me.

With one hand, I crack the lid open. With the other, I toss in the envelopes and jump back before the lid snaps shut like a triggered rat trap. Big Blue Biter likes fingers.

The post office has fixed it a bunch of times, but the repairs never last. Its appetite is insatiable. Legend has it that one time it devoured an entire arm.

I laugh at Big Blue Biter's failed attempt to eat me and hoof it to the guitar shop, my favorite place in the entire world.

I'm going to be a professional guitarist someday. I just haven't decided what kind yet. Maybe I'll join a metal band and be a guitar hero playing five-minute solos. Or maybe I'll be a singer-songwriter and play songs about lonesome nights or whatever. Most of those guys have beards, so I'll have to learn how to grow facial hair. Whatever kind of guitarist I am, I'll need to practice a lot and get really good. Fortunately, I like practice. It makes me concentrate on what I'm doing with my fingers. How they move. What color they are. What shape they are. How many of them I have. Playing guitar helps me pass as human, and after today I really need the practice.

Dozens of guitars hang from hooks on the wall: acoustics and electrics, solid bodies, hollow bodies, semi-hollow bodies, six-strings, twelve-strings, new, used.

I pause in front of my dream guitar: a blue-sparkle Fender Stratocaster. And there's my other dream guitar: a Martin acoustic mahogany Dreadnought. And my other, other dream guitar: a Gibson Flying V in fire-engine red.

I have a lot of dreams.

My own guitar is a humble, battered acoustic I bought with the family discount, since Dale is Mom's cousin.

I named it Stringy.

A framed photo behind the counter shows Dale with his old glam metal band. His hair is poofy and he's stuffed into leopard-print tights. He looks super dorky, but the expression on his face as he rips into a blazing solo is pure happiness.

I know where the photo was taken, because Dale's told me about sixteen thousand times. His band, Eërbleëd, got to open for a bigger band at Desert Sky Pavilion, the outdoor amphitheater just outside Cedar Creek View. He played for twenty thousand people, and it was the best moment of his life.

Another one of my dreams is to play on that stage before a crowd of screaming masses.

Only I won't be wearing leopard-print tights.

And hopefully by then I'll have full control over my shifting so I don't transform into a giant squid in front of my fans. Screaming at a concert is good, but not that kind of screaming.

I head into the back room. Dale is bent over his workbench, doing something with a screwdriver to an electric guitar.

"Hey, Dale," I say. No answer.

"Dale," I say a little louder.

"DALE!"

He finally looks up. "Hey, dude!" His long hair is de-poofed and he's in his standard uniform of ripped jeans and a weathered metal T-shirt. Today's T-shirt is Anthrax, which is both the name of a band and a deadly disease you can catch from sheep.

We go into a glass-walled practice room with Dale's motto stenciled on the window: *You Gotta Shed if You Want to Shred*. "To shed" means putting in a lot of time to learn and practice. "To shred" means to play superfast and awesome.

I break Stringy out of my gig bag and tune up.

"Why the long face, dude?"

Oh, god, what is my face doing now? How long is it?

Wait. That's not what he means.

"It's just . . . there's a lot going on."

"You have stress? With a guitar in your hands? The keys to freedom? The starship that'll take you anywhere your mind can fathom? And you still have stress?"

"Yeah."

"That sounds bad. Play something."

I go through some scales.

Dale closes his eyes and inhales as if he's smelling the notes. He frowns. "Play something else."

I finger-pick some patterns, playing all the notes, in time, with good tone, but Dale crosses his arms and shakes his head.

"You sound really pent-up. Like, all tight and clenched."

Who wouldn't be clenched when they're afraid their fingers might shift into spider legs? Clenching seems like the right thing to do under the circumstances.

"Let's try something else." Dale heads into the front room and comes back with an electric guitar. It's not one of my dream guitars, but it's beautiful, a cherry Epiphone SG. There's a huge buzz when he plugs it into an amp.

"Play."

I settle the guitar over my leg, wrap my left hand around the neck, grip a pick between the thumb and forefinger of my right hand and position it over the strings. And I have no idea what to play.

"Do what your fingers tell you," Dale coaches.

My fingers tell me, "We promise to remain fingers. We will not turn into claws or tentacles."

I strike a power chord. *KA-CHOOOOOWWWWW.* The sound pummels the room and rattles the walls.

Dale grins. "That's more like it. I love a good G on an electric guitar. It's a kick in the chest. It's like riding a wild elephant. But remember, it's not the instrument, it's the song. Try something simpler. Just a single note."

I put my finger down on the D string, fifth fret, and strike it with my pick. *WAAAAAAAAAANNNG.*

"Yeah!" Dale says. "Now just hold that note. Bend it. Listen to it. Let it ring."

I bend the string up and the note climbs higher, giving me a nice, distorted scream. The guitar and the amp sound great together, but they're not controlling me, I'm controlling them. My mind and my heart travel through my hands, into the guitar, and out the speaker.

When the note finally fades and dies, I feel better than I have in months.

Dale nods with approval. "That's what happens when you forget yourself. When you forget where you are. When you forget everything that bugs you. You forget the gravity holding you to the planet. And then, young dude? Then, you are truly free."

    Which sounds great.

    Unless you lose focus.

    Unless you lose control of your body.

    Unless your hand grows feathers.

    Stressed and clenched again, I give back the guitar.

# CHAPTER 4

**CEDAR CREEK VIEW LIES TEN** miles from the bright lights of Phoenix, so our night sky is inky black. Sitting on the roof of my house with Growler snuggled in my lap, I stare up at the stars. "Which one do you think it is, Growler?"

I whisper, because I don't want my parents to know I'm up here.

Growler growls. She's a nine-pound terrier mix composed of messy black-and-tan fur and an active, fluffy tail. I'd describe her personality as both angry and cuddly.

I point at another star. "How about that one? That's Upsilon Andromedae. It's forty-four light-years away. That means it would take a beam of light forty-four years to get from there to here, and that's traveling at 186,000 miles per second. Can you even imagine that?"

Growler is too busy growling at her own leg to wonder at the marvels of the universe.

I've never stopped wondering. Because somewhere out there in all the cosmos is my origin story.

When I was little I asked my parents where babies come from.

They gave each other weird looks, and after a while Mom cleared her throat. "Jake, you fell to Earth in a flaming blob of goo."

Dad nodded. "The neighborhood was still under construction. There were a lot of vacant lots around our house, so we were the only ones who saw you land. We ran a few hundred yards into the desert and expected to find a smoking crater. Instead, there was goo. Goo and you."

According to Mom and Dad, I was a shapeless little puddle. Kind of like a big loogie. They didn't know what I was, or even if I was alive.

Mom worried I might be toxic and wanted to call the fire department. Dad wanted to poke me with his shoe.

But then I made a noise.

I cried.

My cry didn't sound like a human baby's, more like air flapping out a balloon, but it was enough that Dad gave up the idea of kicking me. Instead, he leaned over and very gently touched me with his finger.

"You changed, then," Mom said. "Right in front of our eyes. Like a magic trick. Or a special effect. Or a miracle. You changed into you, Jake. You changed into our baby boy."

So they did the only thing they could think of. They freaked out.

They also picked me up and swaddled me in Dad's jacket. Freaking out but with love in their hearts, they carried me home.

I keep looking at the stars and thinking.


Agnes doesn't want to talk about her "analysis of Goo Specimen Number One" at school. She thinks it would be much more effective to show me instead. After some quick texts during Physical Wellness, she wrangles her mom into wrangling my mom, and suddenly we have a playdate scheduled at Agnes's house after school.

"We are not calling it a playdate," I say, breathing hard as we run around the track.

Adrian and Eirryk peel themselves off the pack jogging

in front of us. "Playdate, ha ha ha," says Adrian.

"Ha ha ha," agrees Eirryk, as if "ha ha ha" qualifies as an actual joke.

Adrian makes finger quotes. "'Play,' ha ha ha."

"'Date,'" Eirryk contributes.

"I'm gonna finish the lap," Agnes announces. She shifts into another gear and sprints ahead, leaving me, Adrian, Eirryk, and the rest of the entire class in her dust.

"You trying out for swim team, Wind?" Eirryk asks.

When did I become "Wind" to him? I used to be Jake.

"Nah."

Since the day of my ear-to-ear grin in the grocery store, I've been paying a lot of attention to faces. Surprise shows on Eirryk's. Maybe even a tiny hint of disappointment. But his words don't match. "Did you forget how to swim over the summer?"

I used to be good at sports. I could always stretch a little farther to catch the Nerf ball that even kids older and taller than me couldn't reach. And maybe I wasn't able to pump my legs the fastest, but I could stretch my stride to win any footrace. And in a swimming pool? I can't turn myself into a dolphin, but a tiny bit of webbing between the toes isn't too hard.

But it feels wrong.

A lot of being good at sports comes from putting in hours and hours of practice. Everything worth doing takes hard work. You gotta shed if you want to shred. But aren't most pro basketball players taller than average? Doesn't having bigger hands help them with ball handling? Some of the best long-distance bike racers have big hearts. It helps them pump more blood and send more oxygen to their muscles.

How is that any different from growing webbed feet when you need them?

I don't know.

But I do know it *is* different.

And knowing changes everything.

So, even without the Hums and sinkholes and bird hands, I won't do competitive sports anymore.

Also, it'd be really bad to turn into a seal in the middle of swim meet.

"I'm too busy," I tell Adrian and Eirryk.

"He's got a girlfriend," Adrian explains to Eirryk, as if they haven't been laughing at me for hanging out with Agnes since school began.

Adrian speeds up. For a few seconds, it's just me and Eirryk, running side by side. Maybe without Adrian around,

Eirryk and I can go back to being friends.

But then Eirryk says, "You changed."

He catches up to Adrian, and then I'm running alone.

Mom drives me to Agnes's house, even though the Oakeses only live four blocks away. She wants to make sure I don't have fish scales or spider eyes or a tapioca face if I'm hanging out with a friend.

Agnes's house looks almost exactly like ours: two stories, stucco-coated, sand-colored. The only difference is the Oakeses have a prickly pear cactus in front while we have a big saguaro.

I press the doorbell, trying to wave my mom off, who's still waiting at the curb with the engine idling. A woman in a blue T-shirt and black yoga pants opens the door. She smiles in a warm and confident way.

"Jake! I'm Dolores." I catch her giving my mom a thumbs-up. Mom returns the thumb and drives off. Just to be sure, I check to make sure I still only have two thumbs.

Agnes's living room is the same as my family's living room, only less cluttered. There's no big, sprawling sofa like we have, just a two-cushion love seat and a couple of chairs. The corner off the kitchen is outfitted with a desk and a computer and a stack of real estate flyers. On the wall where we have a TV, they have shelves with books, plants, and framed photos. Most of them are of Agnes and her mom. One of them is a selfie with a third person in it, a man with a nose that reminds me of Agnes's. Agnes's mom looks a little younger in the picture than she does now, and Agnes is a toddler. They're outside with Christmas trees in the background. The man is holding a saw. They're happy and smiling.

Ms. Oakes—Dolores—gives me a chocolate-chip cookie. The chocolate chips are the perfect degree of gooey. A little gooey is fine when it's confined to a cookie.

"Agnes, Jake is here!" she bellows. I'm surprised the windows don't shatter. At a more normal volume she says, "Sorry, sometimes it's hard to get Agnes's attention."

"Oh, sure, okay, I—"

"AGNES!!!!"

There's still no sign of Agnes, so Dolores supplies me with another cookie to give to Agnes and directs me upstairs.

I find Agnes in her room, doing push-ups with a book spread on the floor.

"Forty-five," she grunts. "Forty-six . . ."

"Uh, hey, Agnes."

"Hey, Jake. Can you turn the page for me? Forty-seven. Forty-eight."

I crouch and flip the page. It's a biology textbook opened to a chapter on genetics. It looks pretty advanced. High school, at least.

"Thanks. Forty-nine. Fifty. I do push-ups until I finish a chapter or my arms give out, whichever comes first. Fifty-one. Fifty-two. Don't eat my cookie."

While Agnes continues to read and torture herself, I nibble my own cookie and glance around her room. The layouts of our houses are identical, and Agnes has the same room I do, only with a color scheme limited to black and white and grays—Night Kite's colors. She has a steel desk with a microscope, a stack of paper maps, and a rack of glass flasks and vials and beakers. A set of hand weights sits under her desk next to a coiled jump rope.

I've totally got her figured out.

"You're trying to turn yourself into Night Kite."

Agnes scoffs between push-ups. "Night Kite is a comic book character. She lives in a mansion atop her own private mountain. Sixty-three. I just read and study and work out every day, including strength training and martial arts.

Sixty-four. I practice Shaolin Kung Fu at the Shady Leaf Plaza shopping center. I'm a green belt. Sixty . . . five. And I'm taking an online class in crime detection while I perfect the design of a lethal slingshot."

"You are totally trying to turn yourself into Night Kite."

"Sixty-six. Sixty . . . seven."

She collapses on her belly with a disappointed "Ugh."

"Sixty-seven push-ups is pretty good," I assure her.

"It's not good enough."

"Not good enough for what?"

"To be Night Kite, okay? You were right. I'm trying to be Night Kite. I know, I'm weird."

"The crime-fighting part is maybe weird, but making yourself supersmart and superstrong is cool. You could end up being a professional athlete or an astronaut or something."

Agnes leaps to her feet. "I don't want to be an athlete or an astronaut. I want to be Night Kite. I mean, I won't use that name. I need my own name. And I'll never be a billionaire. Night Kite inherited her fortune from her parents. My mom's barely a thousandaire."

Agnes doesn't mention a dad. I'm curious, especially

after seeing the family picture on the shelf, but I don't like it when people pry into my own secrets, so I don't ask.

Agnes picks up the jump rope and starts swinging and hopping. I flinch to avoid getting hit with the rope. "What do your parents do?" she asks between jumps.

"My mom does marketing stuff at a soap company. She tries to get people to feel emotional about soap. And my dad is a doctor of butts."

"You mean a proctologist?"

"That's what I just said."

She laughs, which I like. She gets my humor.

"Let's look at goo." She puts down the rope and moves over to the microscope. It's old and heavy, like an ancient piece of factory equipment.

"You have your own Night Scope." That's what Night Kite calls her microscope.

"I got this from a thrift shop," Agnes says, proud. "It was in really bad shape, but I taught myself how to fix it up. Have a look."

There's already a glass slide in place, clamped down by flat little strips of metal. I bend down to peer through the eyepiece.

I expect the goo to look like goo under a microscope.

But it's much more complicated than simple goo. It changes colors. Blood-red, ice blue, tropical-parrot green. And it changes shape: a circle, then a sharp-edged star, then lengthening into a strand, then contracting into a pinpoint, then expanding out again like an ink stain.

Is that what's going on inside me when I shift?

"This is just a small sample from what I collected at school. The rest of it is in the back of the refrigerator in a cup filled with dirt. If it can survive underground, I'm sure it'll be fine."

"Your mom doesn't mind?"

"No, I keep all kinds of specimens in there. She learned to leave them alone after the scorpion incident. Anyway, it won't be there long. Tomorrow I'm going to pack it in dry ice and mail it to a biology professor at Arizona State University."

I clench myself real tight. "Maybe we should keep this to ourselves," I say, trying not to sound like a person clenched real tight.

"Why? They have an entire research department over there. Lab equipment, chemical testing stuff, DNA sequencers, an electron microscope—"

"*Night Kite* number 83," I say, thinking fast.

"The Star Hammer crossover?"

"Right. Remember, she found a shard of Star Hammer's hammer hand and sent it to Doctor Krudd at Galaxy Labs for analysis, but—"

"Doctor Krudd used the shard to clone Star Hammer and the clone destroyed half of Glimmer City and then Night Kite and the real Star Hammer got into an epic battle that destroyed the other half of Glimmer City."

"Right."

"And that's your argument for not sending the goo to a university research lab?"

"Exactly."

"There's just one problem."

Only one? "What's that?"

"This situation is nothing like *Night Kite* number 83."

Ugh.

I try another approach: "But won't it be more fun if we investigate this ourselves?"

Agnes strokes her chin. "I guess handling this on our own would be good training."

I nod with energy. "Totally, it would!"

Agnes claps her hands once. "Okay. So, we'll keep our ears out for word of more sinkholes. And when we hear about the next one, we investigate. We might have to do some extreme things. Are you prepared to do extreme things, Jake?"

I don't know what she means by "extreme," but I'm relieved she's not going to reveal the existence of goo to a bunch of strangers, so I agree to go along with whatever she wants.

I'm sure there's no possible way this could turn out to be a mistake.

# CHAPTER 5

**DAD TALKS ABOUT BUTTS WHILE** spooning a pile of steaming fried rice onto my plate. I'm trying not to pay attention to him for reasons that should be obvious, but every now and again words like "extraction" and "inflammation" leak through.

I raise my hand like I'm in school. "May I eat dinner in my room, please?"

"No," Mom says, "but if you stay at the table with us your father promises to stop talking about rear ends."

Dad hands me my plate. "I make no promises. Sharing my work with family is very important to me. Besides, nasi goreng is not to be eaten alone."

Nasi goreng is spicy Indonesian fried rice. Both my

parents are Dutch-Indonesian, which means their families are part Dutch and part Indonesian. Neither Mom nor Dad has ever been to Holland or Indonesia, but food reminds them of home, even though it's a home they've never been to.

I wonder what people on my planet eat. I wonder if there's some food on Earth that could make me feel closer to my original home.

Mom's talking about emotional soap to keep Dad from talking about butts when the doorbell bing-bongs.

Mom and Dad look at each other, tense jaws, tight frowns. That's their reaction anytime someone unexpected shows up at our door, because of *they*.

Mom and Dad both get up to answer. I hang back to spy.

Peeking around the corner, I see a tall white woman through the cracked-open door. Her hair is neat, her clothes are neat, her face is neat, and even her voice is neat. "I'm so sorry to bother your family, and I'm not selling anything or asking for donations—"

"We're in the middle of dinner," my mom interrupts. Mom usually has welcoming manners, but she can turn them off whenever she wants.

The neat woman smiles. "Then I won't take more than a few seconds of your time. I'm with a private research firm investigating the sinkholes plaguing Cedar Creek View, and I'm reaching out to residents and asking them to contact us if they experience any odd occurrences."

Mom and Dad both relax their shoulders.

"A private research firm?" Dad asks.

The woman hands him a business card. "The Collaboratory," she says. "We're providing our services to the city to investigate and hopefully prevent new holes."

Dad reads the card. "Dr. Claudia Woll, Project Director. I'm a doctor myself, you know."

"Oh, what kind?"

"A proctologist," he says, proudly.

"How wonderful," Woll says. "Have you encountered any holes close up?"

Dad opens his mouth to say something.

"She means sinkholes," Mom interrupts. "No, we haven't seen any close up. There was one at our son's school, though."

"Oh? Cedar Creek View Middle School? Is your son home? Would it be okay if I talked to him?"

"He wasn't nearby when it happened. He just heard

other kids talking about it. Mostly rumors and exaggerations, I imagine."

I wince. That's the lie I told my parents. Hearing them repeat my lie makes it worse.

"Those holes are really becoming a problem," Dad says.

"A big problem," Woll agrees. "But we hope to get to the bottom of it, so to speak."

Bottom, ha. Not a bad butt joke.

Dad appreciates it. "That's outstanding!"

Mom shakes her head at him. "We're happy the city has you looking into it. I wish we could be of help."

"Well, if you happen to come across a sinkhole, please contact me. You have my card. Thank you so much for your time."

We go back to dinner.

Mom talks about soap, and Dad talks about butts. I move my fork around my fried rice. It's a good thing this Dr. Woll person is looking into the sinkholes, but since I'm somehow connected to them, I want to figure out what's going on before she does.

After dinner I charge upstairs to my room. Growler is happy to see me, which she expresses by growling from under the bed. I grab my phone to text Agnes, but there's already a message from her: "Someone came to our house asking about sinkholes."

"Same here," I text back. "Dr. Claudia Woll from the Collaboratory. Did you tell her about the sinkhole at school?"

"Yeah."

I swallow and type, "What did you say?"

Instead of texting back, she calls.

"I told her there was a big sinkhole at school and I was right there when it opened up," she says before hello.

"Did you tell her about me?"

"Tell her what about you?"

"Anything. What did you say about me?"

"You're being weird. Why are you being weird?"

It's a fair question, but not one I want to answer.

What would Woll do if she found out I was a goo boy from another planet? I envision military complexes out in the desert. Guards with machine guns. Barbed wire. Containment cells. White operating rooms with gleaming steel instruments.

A whole bunch of *they*.

I am being paranoid.

If Woll is investigating the sinkholes, and if the

sinkholes have something to do with me and the problems I'm having with shifting, then maybe we should help Woll out.

"I told Woll that everybody at school saw the sinkhole and ran over to check it out," Agnes says. "That's all."

"Oh. Okay."

"I didn't mention the goo, if that's what you're worried about."

"Good. Yeah. I want to keep the investigation between the two of us."

"I know. Because it's more fun that way."

"Right."

"But are you sure? We want to figure out what's going on, and Woll wants to figure out what's going on. We could help each other."

"Maybe later. But for now, just the two of us. Okay?"

There's a long pause before Agnes says, "Okay."

# CHAPTER 6

**THE NEXT COUPLE OF DAYS** pass without anything interesting or alarming happening. No Hum. No accidental shifting. No sinkholes. Things are boring. I like it.

It doesn't last.

I wake up with the Hum in my head and my skin feeling like applesauce. Growler growls while I inspect my body. Two legs, two arms, normal amount of thumbs. So far I'm holding myself together.

So far.

My phone buzzes.

"Agnes? It's 3:40 in the morning." My voice doesn't squelch, which I take as a good sign.

"There's something you need to see," she says.

I sit up. "School's in"—I'm too bleary to do the math—"a whole bunch of hours."

"It's urgent. You have to come now."

"Why are you even awake?"

"I couldn't sleep, so I went out on patrol."

"Does that mean you snuck out and rode your bike around the neighborhood?"

"That's what I just said. There's a new sinkhole, and I'm the only one who knows about it. We have to check it out before the site's swarming with city workers and cops and Dr. Woll."

I need to be firm with her. There's no way I'm sneaking out. "If my parents caught me I'd be spending the rest of the school year in my bedroom, twenty-four/seven."

"You won't be gone more than a few minutes. It's on 35 Redwood Drive."

I know that address. It's just around the corner.

Twelve years ago, when the neighborhood was mostly just desert, that's where I splashed down.

A sinkhole.

Right where I arrived on Earth.

"I'll be there in five minutes."

I throw on some jeans and a T-shirt and shoes and a hoodie.

Growler growls.

"You think this is a bad idea? Going out during a Hum?"

Growler growls.

"You think it's a *good* idea?"

Growler growls.

"You think knowing how to multiply fractions will be useful later in life?"

Growler growls.

It must be nice to be confident in all your opinions.

Out my window I go, down the drainpipe, down the paloverde tree, feeling more like I'm dripping than climbing, until my feet touch the backyard paving stones. Creeping to the sidewalk like an escaped inmate, I expect to be pinned by blinding floodlights and stopped by armed guards. But there're only some distant coyote howls and the rumble of air conditioners.

Agnes waits for me in the dark in front of 35 Redwood Drive. An SUV sits in the driveway.

"The hole's in the backyard," she whispers.

"Why are you peeping into people's backyards?"

"Crimes don't always conveniently happen in front yards, Jake."

Thirty-five Redwood Drive looks like every other house in the neighborhood: sand-colored stucco and a gravel front yard with decorative cacti.

We peer over the low concrete-block wall, into the backyard. It's scattered with typical backyard stuff: a hammock, a little kid's bicycle, a basketball, fallen fruit from a grapefruit tree. And a sinkhole. It's not all that great of a sinkhole, maybe big enough to swallow a BBQ grill. But it's fresh. Clumps of grass and dirt crumble off the edge.

"I wonder who lives here."

Agnes consults her notebook.

"Albert and Maria Foster, and their daughter Maya, six years old."

"How do you know that? Wait, don't tell me. The less I know, the less I'll have to tell the cops when they arrest us for trespassing."

Agnes gets out a plastic cup. "Let's collect some soil samples."

We hop over the wall and tiptoe toward the hole. I manage only a few steps when the Hum dials up the power.

It's even worse than it was in my room, like swallowing a power drill.

"Are you okay?" Agnes says. "You look weird."

I check my fingers and feel my face. "What do you mean, weird?"

"Like, pale. Are you going to puke?"

Actually, I feel like I'm made of puke. "I'm fine."

She cocks her head. She knows I'm not fine. She knows I'm lying.

"Sometimes . . . sometimes I hear a hum," I find myself telling her. "The Hum, is what I call it. It's deep and low, and nobody else can hear it. I know, it sounds really—"

"Annoying?"

I was going to say "suspicious," but I like Agnes's conclusion better. "Yeah, annoying. It makes me feel sick to my stomach sometimes. That's all."

Agnes gets a bottle of water and a washcloth out of her backpack. She pours some water onto the cloth.

"You need a cold compress. Put this on your forehead."

The cool, wet cloth doesn't help with the Hum, but it does feel nice.

She looks down the hole for a while.

She's going to figure out the connection between the Hum and my shifting.

She's going to learn that I'm an alien.

She's going to know I'm a big loogie.

A blob of goo bursts from the hole, arcing through the air and landing in a sploogey puddle. It's the size of a large pizza, but it's not anything I'd ever want to eat, bubbling and pulsating and convulsing as if it's alive and in pain.

Agnes lurches toward it with her sample cup out, but I grab her arm to hold her back.

"Leave it alone!" I say. I don't know why, exactly. I just know she shouldn't touch it.

"Discovery entails risk," Agnes says, doing some kind of jujitsu maneuver to free herself from my grip. But she hangs back when the goo starts shivering, mirroring the sensation in my belly from the Hum.

The glob shoots out in a long gooey tentacle and lands with a splash against the Fosters' back door. It grows a thin tendril, probing the doorknob, and then it slurps itself through the keyhole like a spaghetti noodle.

"Whoa," Agnes says.

"Whoa," I totally agree.

"C'mon, let's get a closer look." We sneak up to the

window to spy inside. The goo puddles on the kitchen floor, glistening in the glow of the oven clock. It wiggles in beat with my own heart.

Agnes starts rummaging through her backpack and pulls out a set of lockpicks.

"You are not going inside."

"Why not? I thought you wanted to investigate the goo. If we're not going to do it, it's going to be Dr. Woll. You want her to have all the fun?"

I sigh. "Fine. Pick the lock."

Agnes beams as if I've just given her a birthday present.

She's about to get to work when the kitchen lights snap on. A woman stands with a toilet plunger, and through the window, I can make out some muffled curse words about plumbing problems. This must be Maria Foster. Frowning, she sleepily stumbles over to the kitchen sink. She's almost there when she notices the pulsating blob of goo spread over the floor. Her frown deepens. She takes a cautious step toward it.

"No!" I shout. "Don't touch it!"

She lets out a startled shriek as the goo springs at her.

The blob washes over Maria's feet, climbs up her calves, stretches up her middle, crawls up her neck, pours into her screaming mouth. Her fingers desperately claw at her face as the goo spreads across her cheeks and covers her eyes. In a few seconds, Maria Foster is just a vaguely human-shaped statue covered in goo.

A man with bedhead rushes in. This must be Albert Foster.

Agnes works frantically on the lock while goo-slathered Maria Foster reaches out with dripping fingers and clutches Albert Foster's shoulders. He flounders backward, trying to push his goo-wife away, but the goo spreads over him, sealing his eyes, filling his mouth, flowing over every square inch of him.

And then Maya Foster, their little girl, enters the kitchen.

"Kid, run!" I scream.

She's smart enough to do what I say.

But she's not fast enough.

She only gets a few steps before her goo-parents descend upon her.

And now, the goo family is complete.

The door lock clicks. "Got it!" says Agnes.

"Agnes, do not go in there."

Something in the tone of my voice convinces Agnes not

to argue with me. Or maybe it's just Agnes showing some common sense. Even if she really were Night Kite, she'd have no defense against an aggressive blob.

Splooting and bubbling, the goo takes on the form of the Fosters, right down to the shapes of their noses and the color of their skin. If I got close to them, I bet I'd see every strand of hair in place. I bet their fingerprints would be right. But something tells me these aren't the Fosters. Not the real Fosters anymore. These are goo Fosters.

Maria Goo Foster takes the plunger and sticks it in the oven.

Albert Goo Foster grabs a handful of forks from a drawer. He drops them into the sink and hits a switch. The garbage disposal sounds miserable as it tries to eat metal.

Maya Goo Foster takes a can of Whizzy Cheese from the refrigerator, squirts almost all of it into the microwave, and sets the timer for twenty minutes.

"They don't know how kitchens work," I observe.

Agnes takes some notes. "Nope."

"What are we actually witnessing here?"

"It's an invasion," Agnes says. "Or a takeover. Or another kind of bad thing. It's . . . awful."

For once, there's no excitement, or glee, or determination

in Agnes's eyes. They look haunted. This isn't fun.

I have to shut my eyes to conceal what I'm feeling.

The goo did something monstrous. It *is* a monster. And I'm made of goo. So what does that make me?

The glow of headlights catches my eye. On the other side of the backyard wall, a white van comes to a stop at the curb.

There are no markings on the van.

Everybody knows unmarked vans are bad news.

Two people climb out of the front seat, dressed in baggy, one-piece white outfits with boots and gloves. Their heads are fully covered by hoods with built-in goggles.

"Hazmat suits," Agnes whispers. "For avoiding exposure to hazardous materials."

"Considering what happened to the Fosters, that seems like a good idea."

Forlorn, Agnes looks inside her backpack. "We need some hazmat suits. I wonder how much they cost."

I want to be encouraging and suggest that Agnes is probably handy enough to make her own hazmat suit, but when the two people in actual hazmat suits start climbing over the wall into the backyard, I make a quick dash to hide behind a patch of ocotillo cacti.

Agnes chooses not to hide with me. She does a crouching-running sort of thing on nimble feet, sticking to shadows and sneaking around the grapefruit tree. She manages to get over the wall without the hazmat people seeing her.

Total Night Kite maneuver.

She turns to me and makes a bunch of hand gestures that could mean "stay still and watch" or "I am bouncing a ball and now I'm poking you in the eyes with two fingers."

The hazmat pair edges up to the hole.

"How old?" asks one of them.

The other one jabs the screen of a tablet with a stylus. "Geological outgassing indicates no more than forty minutes."

I don't know what geological outgassing is, but I bet Agnes does.

"Presence of xenogel?" asks the first.

I bet I *do* know what xenogel is. It's the goo.

"I'll tell you as soon as I know, Tami. You don't have to ask."

"Asking is part of protocol, Leonard. I ask; you tell. That's how it works."

"I have a question. What is Tami's most annoying habit?

Take your time; I know you have a lot to choose from."

"Is this about lunch? Those were good burritos."

"It was chopped baloney and broccoli in a tortilla. That's not a burrito."

"John's Burritos was recently voted the Most Interesting Burrito Restaurant in the Phoenix metropolitan area."

Leonard talks to the sky. "Baloney and broccoli is a crime against burritos. It's a burrito crime."

"Is there xenogel or isn't there?"

Leonard consults his tablet again. "Five hundred forty-eight grams, pre-shift. But it's out of the hole."

Tami says a bad word. "We're too late."

"What are we supposed to do now? Contain the results?"

"We don't have facilities for that. We just file a report and let a vacuum crew handle it."

"That could take a while. They've been busy."

Tami shrugs, and they both head back to the van. Soon, taillights recede down the road.

I stand in the cool night air and breathe. That was all a lot to take in. I'm looking around for Agnes when the end of a rope drops in front of my face. Agnes slides down the rope from the roof.

Her landing is . . . just okay. I can tell by her frown that she's not satisfied with it.

"Why are you playing with rope?" I whisper-hiss at her. "And why did you leave me alone with the hazmat creeps? And what's geological outgassing?"

"I was avoiding detection while planting a tracking device on their van," Agnes whispers back, trying to sound like it's something she does every day, but I can tell she's really excited about getting to do Night Kite stuff.

"A tracking device? That's a real thing?"

"Sure. You just take the GPS unit out of your mom's phone, tape it to a magnet, and then spend a month doing extra chores because you broke your mom's phone. But totally worth it!"

She shows me her own phone. A little red dot moves along a map.

I give her a respectful nod. "So we figure out where the hazmat creeps are going and where they hang out, and then maybe we can find some answers. Also, you rappelled from the roof just to show off, admit it."

"How'd my landing look?"

I'm about to answer, but noises come from the kitchen.

"We fester," says a little girl's voice.

"Yes," agrees a man. "We are the Festers."

"Fosters," a woman corrects. "We are the Fosters, and we are having family time in the ketchup."

"Kitten," the man says.

"Kitchen," the little girl corrects.

A dish shatters, and someone laughs.

# CHAPTER 7

**SATURDAY MORNING IS DOBUTT MORNING,** a family tradition that means we get up early and Dad bakes oatmeal donuts. Oats are good for butts, apparently. Therefore, Dobutt morning.

Mom's on the phone in the kitchen while Dad interrogates me about school.

"How's Eirryk?" he says around a mouthful of dobutt.

I shrug. "I haven't seen him much. I don't think we're friends anymore."

Dad frowns, concerned, like he's diagnosing a patient.

"That happens a lot between elementary school and middle school. A lot of things start changing at your age. Maybe that's why your shifting went a little wonky over the summer. Maybe you're not so different from other boys after all." He takes another thoughtful bite. "But what about Agnes Oakes? Seems like you're spending a lot of time with her."

"Not that much." I haven't told Mom and Dad about the hazmat creeps last night. Part of me wants to pretend it never happened. The goo—the xenogel—did horrible things to the Fosters. And if I'm made of the same xenogel . . .

My phone shudders once in my pocket.

It's a text from Agnes: "Say yes."

Mom emerges from the kitchen. "That was Dolores Oakes on the phone. She wants to know if Jake would like to accompany her and Agnes to the mall."

I haven't been to the mall since before summer. Too many people there. Too big a chance I'll expose myself in another ear-to-ear grin.

"Yes," I say.

Forty minutes later—after answering a lot of Dad's questions regarding itching, burning, and wriggling—I'm walking through the main entrance of Cedar Creek View Fashion Valley Galleria Mall with Agnes and her mom. Three levels of shops rise to the ceiling of the big, echoey space. Skylights let in way too much Arizona sunshine. It's early, but the mall is already noisy with oontz-oontz music and the footfalls of shoppers.

I used to like it here because of the bookstore and the movie theater, but now it's all too much.

Agnes still hasn't told me why we're at the mall. I don't think it's to see a movie. She tells her mom that she and I want to hang out at the bookstore.

"I will trust your good judgment to remain safe," her mom says. "We'll meet in the food court at noon. That's one hour. Call me if you need anything."

"Yes, Ms. Oakes," I say like someone who never sneaks out at night to witness an entire family being replaced by living goo.

Agnes drags me to the bookstore and commandeers a table in the café.

"I lost track of the hazmat creeps' van somewhere on the south edge of town," she announces, spreading a map of Cedar Creek View on the table. She points to where the van fell off the grid.

"That's the old part of Cedar Creek View. The only stuff out there is a retirement trailer park and the dead mall."

Agnes's eyes get big. "What do you mean 'dead'? Are there zombies?"

"No, just the mall that used to be the mall before this mall."

"Oh," says Agnes, disappointed.

"There's hardly any cell signal out there. That explains why your tracker stopped tracking them."

"Hopefully we'll pick up their trail again."

"Should we check in on the Fosters?"

"I cruised by before sunup," she says. "They were barbecuing."

"Weird time to be doing it, but that doesn't sound hugely weird."

"They were barbecuing milk."

"Oh, well."

"In the meantime, I've done some detecting." Agnes draws a few *X*'s on the map in red marker. "These are sinkholes reported to the city. I'm still trying to hack into the nonpublic records, because there may be more holes they're not telling us about."

"And if that's true, then there might be a lot more . . . xenogel."

"And more people like the Fosters. Blob imposters."

"Imblobsters," I suggest.

"Oh, good name!" Agnes writes something in her notebook. "If we can map out all the sinkholes, maybe we'll see a pattern. Maybe they're all centered on a single location. If we can find that place, maybe we can figure out what's causing them. And if it's all part of some nefarious scheme, we can put a stop to it before we end up with any more imblobsters."

I love how naturally she says "nefarious scheme." It's so Night Kite.

I've been wondering why being Night Kite is so important to her, especially after seeing her in action last night. You can't just do push-ups and read a few books and become a nocturnal bird of justice. You have to be really dedicated to it. You need a reason. Night Kite's origin story starts when her parents are murdered by a corrupt Grimm City police officer. Agnes still hasn't said anything about her father.

I want to know, but it would be rude to ask.

We spend the rest of the hour in the graphic novel section. I page through any story set in outer space, while Agnes reads more *Night Kite*.

We don't say a lot, which is fine. It's nice just to sit

crisscross applesauce with a friend, going through stacks of comics. Eirryk and I would do this sometimes, and I guess I've really missed it. I wish this was my life all the time, just doing normal things, no blanket of dread weighing me down, no secrets to keep, no *they*. Just me and a pal and all the weirdness in the world confined to brightly colored pictures on paper. I wish this could go on forever.

Agnes stands and loops her backpack over her shoulders. "Lunchtime!"

"Pizza? Tacos? Corn dogs?"

She gives it some careful thought. "I vote pizza."

"I meant all three."

Agnes laughs, which is rare for her. "I like the way you think."

On our way to the food court, Agnes talks about microbiology or maybe interrogation techniques or maybe the art of rappelling from roofs when the Hum starts, a big vibrating *WOMMM WOMMM* noise pummeling my head. I look around for a trash can in case I turn entirely liquid and need a receptacle to contain myself in.

"Hey, Jake, are you okay? You look . . . mottled. Is it the Hum?"

"I . . . I . . . Igottagotothebathroom."

I take off at a run, or at least I try to. My legs weigh too much. Am I getting even worse at keeping myself together? That would totally suck since I've already gotten so bad at it.

Heavy and sluggish, I lurch along.

"Jake!" Agnes calls after me. "Do you need a cold compress?"

Color fades. My vision tunnels, and everything farther than a few feet away gets lost in a dark fog. I find the bathrooms more by luck than by sight and stumble inside.

The smells are too strong, lemon cleaner and ammonia. Everything is so bright: the fluorescent lights, reflections off the tile floor, my face in the mirror.

Oh, no. My face.

What have I done to my face?

Eyes like pools of black stare back at me. My nose is a rounded triangle with two wide, vertical nostrils. Short gray-and-black fur covers my face.

With a long, paddle-shaped hand, I shove on the door of the nearest toilet stall.

"Occupied!" grunts an irritated voice.

"Sorry!" I say. It comes out as a moist snuffle.

My whiskers twitch.

*I have whiskers.*

I collapse inside the second toilet stall. There's barely enough space to contain my bulk.

Breathe, Jake, I tell myself.

Try to relax.

Try to focus.

I play guitar scales in my head, imagining my fingers pressing the strings down with precision. But I could never play guitar with these hands, because they're not hands, they're flippers.

My legs fuse into a thick back end.

My body is a big, blubbery mass.

I, Jake Wind, have become a seal.

A seal.

I am an entire seal.

In Arizona, of all places.

On a tide of panic, I burst from the stall, snapping the door off its hinges.

A janitor entering the bathroom takes a swing at me with his mop. I barrel past him out into the wider world of the Saturday mall crowd.

Everybody does what I expect them to do. They hold their phones out at me like vampire hunters with crosses while I gallumph over the shiny floor.

I flop through a blur of legs and faces and noise. There're too many people in my way, pushing and jostling to get a look at me, to gawk and shout.

The only thing worse than shifting into a seal at the mall would be shifting back into human form, right here, in front of everybody, captured by their phone cameras. The world will know about me. *They'll* take me away from my parents. *They'll* put me in a zoo, or some kind of prison for freaks, or a laboratory deep underground where *they'll* perform experiments on their pet alien goo boy.

But then, like a mighty rock splitting a raging river, it's Agnes. She stands with her feet firmly planted, spine straight, shoulders broad, ignoring the chaos around her and focusing her gaze on me.

Our eyes meet. Human to seal.

I want her to recognize me, to see me for who I am. But at the same time, I really, really do not want her to recognize me and see me for who I am.

Calm and controlled, she takes out her phone.

She grips it tight, extends her arm all the way out, and shouts, "I'm going to get some pics!"

The shutter-click of her camera sounds like a tree

cracking in two. Light flashes like a bomb.

But not toward me.

"Hey!" someone screams.

"Watch where you point that!" screams someone else.

Agnes fires off another pic.

Gawkers flinch and throw their arms over their eyes.

"Sorry, new phone," Agnes says. She triggers the flash again and again, blasting the crowd with barrages of blinding light. People cry out in pain and shout nasty words at her. Agnes keeps apologizing and blasting them.

She's doing it on purpose.

And these aren't normal flashes. They are painful and shocking and massively bright. She must have modified her camera, turning it into one of Night Kite's most effective weapons: the Night Kite Light.

Boom, flash, explosions of light, cussing from the crowd, Agnes apologizing but not stopping.

The crowd starts to back away.

She turns to me.

"Shoo, seal," she says.

She doesn't have to say it twice.

I flop my way back into the bathroom and keel over on

my side. I just lie there, trying to catch my breath on the sticky floor.

Gradually, my vision sharpens and color returns. My front flippers separate into fingers. My fur flattens and recedes. The blubber beneath my flesh thins. In a few more seconds, I'm Jake again.

Panting, I fix my hair in the mirror and attempt a smile. It's not good.

I crack the door open and peek outside.

Security guards keep the crowd at a distance while a guy in a tan-and-green uniform with an Animal Control patch on his hat loads a dart in a rifle.

"There's a seal in there!" I scream. "If I hadn't hidden in the toilet stall I bet it would have bitten me and possibly given me rabies!"

The Animal Control guy braves the bathroom, led by the janitor and his menacing mop.

Agnes dodges around the guards and rushes up to me. She hooks me by the arm and drags me away. Nobody's paying much attention to us.

"I'm okay," I tell her. "I didn't get bit."

"I know," she says.

"It was really scary."

"I'm sure."

"I wonder where the seal came from. Or maybe it's a sea lion. I can't tell the difference. I think sea lions are the ones with little earflaps?"

She sighs with impatience. "Jake, I said I *know*. Boy goes into bathroom; seal comes out. Seal goes into bathroom; boy comes out. The seal was you, Jake. You changed into a seal."

I unhook myself from her arm. "I'll take that cold compress now."

# CHAPTER 8

**I'M ON TV. I'M ON** the internet. I'm viral. I'm a meme. I'm #MallSeal.

All the footage is shaky, but there I am, a brown seal snorfling and flopping its way through screaming shoppers at the Cedar Creek View Fashion Valley Galleria Mall.

Most of the news stories treat it like it's funny, but Animal Control is taking it seriously. "We assume the seal was an escaped pet someone was keeping illegally," says the guy from the mall with the hat and tranquilizer gun. "And we would like to remind the public that under the Marine Mammal Protection Act of 1972, seals, sea lions, walruses and other pinnipeds cannot be kept without a federal permit."

After the seal story, there's a piece about a sinkhole that formed in the mall parking lot. It's a big hole, but after the whole seal thing nobody seems to care much about it.

"And you were in the bathroom the whole time?" Dad says, yet again. It's been a few hours since Agnes's mom dropped me off, and I've spent all that time talking to my parents to assure them I'm okay.

"Yeah. I really had to go. Must have been those dobutts."

"And you didn't even see the seal?"

"I heard some weird sounds from the stall next over, but I really didn't want to know what was causing them."

"Understandable," Mom says. "I'm just glad you and Agnes and Dolores are okay. I'm terrified to think what could have happened to you."

"Yeah, phew, thank god we're all okay."

Mom's face turns red. Dad's turns a little redder.

"You're not okay," Mom says, her voice tight. "Give us some credit. *You were the seal.*"

I open my mouth. Dad points a rigid finger at me. "Don't lie to us, Jake. Don't make this worse. How long have you been turning into animals?"

Am I going to tell them about the bird hand on the first

day of my very first class?

"This is the first time anything like this has ever happened," I claim.

Dad pinches his nose.

Mom blows air out of hers.

They exchange looks for a long time, having a silent conversation.

"You're done going to school, " Mom says.

"You're done going anywhere," Dad says.

My heart falls into a pit deeper than any sinkhole.

"This won't happen again! I promise! It was only once. The mall was too crowded. Everything was too bright. That's what triggered the shift. I won't go to the mall again. Or anywhere with too many people."

The argument lasts an entire hour.

The words "trust," "judgment," and "responsibility" are uttered at least three billion times. And through it all, the dark threat of *they* looms large.

There's not much I can say in my own defense.

They have some more silent conversation with each other, negotiating with eyebrow raises, shaking heads, and nods.

"Restricted," Mom says, finally, and a dark cloud descends.

No outings on my own.

No hanging out with Agnes after school, even though I tell them a dozen times that Agnes and her mom saw nothing, which is at least half true.

Mom will drop me off at school in the mornings, and Dad will pick me up.

"What about guitar lessons?"

They *can't* take that away from me. They know how much guitar means to me. They have to let me keep going to guitar.

Dad crosses his arms. "No guitar lessons."

My heart—or whatever solidified goo structure in my chest functions like a heart—dies a cold death of despair.

"Well, hold on," says Mom. "It's not fair to take money away from Dale. And he's family."

Dad squeezes his eyes shut. He looks like he has a headache. They both do. "Okay," he says. "Jake can keep guitar lessons. But I'll take him there and work from the coffee shop across the street, and then we'll go directly home."

"For how long?" I ask.

"For as long as we think it's necessary," Mom says.

When I open my mouth to protest, she shuts me down.

"If you don't like that, it's not too late to pull you out of school."

"I thought home school was for my protection, not for punishment."

"*You were on television, Jake.*"

I know they're right. If the cameras had caught me in the act of shifting . . .

Part of me wants to scream how unfair they're being. Part of me wants to tell them how sorry I am. Part of me wants to thank them for letting me keep guitar lessons. But my throat is too tight to say anything at all. I trudge up to my room to begin serving my sentence.

Agnes calls when I'm sitting on the roof with my guitar and Growler.

"Whatcha doing?" she asks.

"Looking at the stars."

"It's a clear night. There're a lot of them. Deneb is really bright."

"Are you up on your roof, too?"

"Yeah. Climbing and rappelling practice. So, my tracker picked up the hazmat creeps again."

"Let me guess. They were at the sinkhole in the mall parking lot?"

"Yep. About an hour after the . . . incident. I wanted to bike over there and conduct surveillance, but after the . . . incident . . . my mom wouldn't let me out of her sight."

"Ah. Yeah. The incident."

"So, there's probably more xenogel out in the world. Maybe more imblobsters."

I don't know what to say. I don't want to say anything. Cicadas buzz in the dark.

"Looking at any star in particular?" Agnes asks, breaking the silence.

"Nope. Just the whole sky. Wondering where I'm from."

"Ah. So you're an alien. That's what I guessed."

I still can't find words.

"Are we going to talk about what happened today?" Agnes asks.

I should hang up the phone. I should go back inside. I should get under the covers and never come out, not even to eat. Not even to go to the bathroom.

But I stay put and tell Agnes everything.

I tell her how I fell from the sky when I was a baby.

I tell her how my parents found me in the desert.

I tell her that I'm made of goo.

I tell her about my shapeshifting problems.

I tell her everything because she already knows the worst of it, and there's no point in keeping the rest secret. But the real reason I spill is because I feel like I've been holding my breath my entire life. Telling the truth is terrifying, but it feels like I'm breathing for the first time.

"This is amazing! Incredible! Proof of intelligent alien life? Astonishing!" Agnes burbles on like this for a while.

"I'm not that intelligent. I'm only getting C-minuses in pre-algebra. Ms. Yoh says I'm not applying myself, but numbers are really hard."

"Jake, be serious. Knowledge of your existence is a huge advance in our understanding of the universe."

Everything she's saying is true, but I don't like hearing it. It just drives home how weird I am.

"I'm sure this is super fascinating to you, Agnes, but I'm not a specimen."

"No, no. You're right. I'm sorry."

"Thanks. And you can't tell anyone about me."

"Of course not. You're my friend. Your secret is safe with me."

"Promise me?"

"The Night Kite/Star Hammer team-up. Night Kite learns Star Hammer's an alien, and she gives up her life to keep his secret. She comes back to life in the next issue, but that's not the point. She never tells. And I won't either. I promise."

She's quiet for a while. I watch the lights of a plane pass overhead.

"We shouldn't have any secrets," she says, finally. "I know yours. You should know mine."

She takes a breath.

"My dad died when I was four. He was a forklift driver at a warehouse, and some shelves collapsed on him. The company he worked for said it was his fault because he was using his forklift wrong. My mom didn't believe them, so she did a lot of digging and she found a bunch of safety complaints against the company. The brackets that held the shelves in place weren't screwed far enough into the walls. So eventually they broke and fell on my dad and killed him."

She says all this plainly, just reporting the facts, like she's telling me her shoe size. But I hear the smallest quaver in her voice. All these years later, she's still upset. Of course she is. She lost her dad.

"So, your mom found out that the company broke the law, and she made sure people got punished? Which is what Night Kite does?"

"No. The company had more money than we did. A lot more. They hired a huge team of lawyers, and they beat our lawyer. They killed my dad and got away with it."

"That's not right," is all I can think to say. "That's just not right."

"There's nothing I can do about it now. I don't have the knowledge or ability or resources." She pauses. And in that pause, I can hear the cocking of a fist, ready to strike. "But someday."

"Someday," I agree.

I don't know what else to say.

But I do know what to do.

Using my phone's self-timer, I manage to take a selfie with my wrists crossed in the Night Kite signal.

I send it to Agnes.

A few seconds later, she sends one of her doing the signal to me.

And that's it.

Now we're not just friends.

Now we're allies.

# CHAPTER 9

**THE REST OF THE WEEKEND** lasts approximately six thousand years. I never thought I'd look forward to hearing one of Mr. Brown's anti-gum rants in Advisory, but here I am.

"The average person chews three hundred pieces of gum per year. They chew each piece for an average of seven minutes." I still have no idea why he's so down on gum. Maybe gum killed his grandfather. "That's twenty-one hundred minutes! Or thirty-five chewing hours a year! What could you do with your time if you had an extra thirty-five hours each year?"

We all stare blankly at him.

"This is an essay question, people. Get out your writing utensils."

I use my time to draw guitars, because it's Advisory and you can't fail Advisory.

Agnes uses her time to update our to-do list. She shows it to me at lunch. I can't make any sense of it, because she's written it in a secret Agnes code, because of course she has. So she reads it for me:

A. Learn how the Hum and the sinkholes are related to Jake's shapeshifting.

B. Find out what planet Jake is actually from.

C. Help Jake practice shifting into anything at will.

I take a slurp from my juice box and hand her back her list. "Item C is a bad idea."

She blinks, surprised. "Why?"

"Because that means trying to shift. I'm trying to do the opposite."

"*Star Hammer* issue 123, 'Lay Your Hammer Down, O Child of the Cosmos.'"

That's the one where Star Hammer decides the Celestial Mallet is too much responsibility, so he buries it at Earth's core. But then Volcamech attacks the world with magmadroids, and Star Hammer has to give up his new secret identity as a hairstylist to get his hammer back.

"The art on that one was really good."

"The point is," Agnes says slowly, "you have gifts. You should learn how to use them."

"Being hashtag MallSeal is not a gift, Agnes."

"You can change into animals! You can turn to liquid. I would give anything to have your abilities. Instead I have to make do with being awesome at push-ups and good at rope climbing."

"And you're great at those things!"

Agnes takes a breath. Her ears turn a little red. I brace myself, because I sense she's about to unload on me. Mercifully, something else grabs her attention.

"We're being watched," she says. "Blond girl. Blond boy. Blue eyes. Both picking up trash. Boy, about five foot four. Girl, about five foot five and a half. Check your six. That means look behind you."

"I know what 'check my six' means. If they're paying attention to me, I don't want to look at them. Describe them more."

Agnes squints. "The wear on their sneakers indicates they walk on stony surfaces. The boy has a reddish tinge underneath his fingernails. That's soil from the Superstition Mountains. The girl has a small scratch on her right cheek, consistent with the hoof of a mountain goat. Conclusion: They are mountain goat herders."

"You're making that up."

"Yes. Turn around and look at them."

"Don't you have some kind of facial-recognition device loaded with a database of every human on Earth?"

"Not yet," Agnes says with a wistful sigh. "Please just look at them."

"Okay, okay." I turn around, pretending to glance at everything except the twins. Oh, look, it's a tree. And there's a very fine bench. Fascinating. I turn back around.

"They're coming this way. Quick, help me practice my French."

Agnes claps her hands, excited. "I'm going to interrogate them!"

"Bad idea. If they confront me, tell them I'm not Jake."

"For the last time, your 'I'm Marcel from France' plan is the absolute worst."

Fortunately, I have taken the time to learn a little bit of French since the first day of school, which I practice in whispers now: "Un, deux, trois, voila, mon stylo." In

English that's "One, two, three, here is my pen."

Agnes denies me the opportunity to execute my fool-proof garbage plan. "I'm Agnes," she announces. "And this is Jake. Who are you?"

"We are collecting trash," says the boy. He shows us a plastic bag full of empty milk cartons, candy wrappers, some random twigs.

"We are Dairy and Gravy," the girl says.

Agnes and I exchange a look.

"Mary and Davey," the boy corrects. "Forgive our words. We are not from here. We are from—"

I swear, if he says France, I'm going to scream.

"—Dutchland. No. The land of halls. Holland. Yes. We are from Holland."

Agnes jots down some notes. "Are you new?"

The twins make startled little *ulp*s, as if they've been accused of something.

Before they can answer, the bell chimes, signaling the end of lunch.

"That is the signal to flee the outdoors," says Gravy.

"It's the bell," Dairy explains to him. "It means we have to go to class."

That is the most normal thing either one of them has said. But then Dairy adds, "We still study you later," and therefore loses all normal points awarded.

Gravy holds out his plastic bag. "Do you have any trash you wish to dispose of?"

I give Gravy my juice box, and they take off together and melt into the stream of kids heading for class.

Agnes and I watch them go.

"Yeah," she says. "You should definitely stay away from them."

After school, my stressed and busy dad drives me to Dale's Guitar Shed for my lesson. He goes to the coffee shop across the street to do email consultations with patients, and I take refuge in the guitar shop. The air smells of sawdust and burning wires. Power tools whine and buzz from the back room. I go back to see what Dale's up to.

On his workbench lies the biggest electric bass guitar I've ever seen. The body is a massive slab painted with green lizard scales. The neck is as broad as a diving board. I've seen plenty of four-string basses, a couple of five-strings, and pictures of six-strings. This has thirteen. It's ridiculous.

It's bizarre. It's frightening. It's amazing.

Dale's bent over the bass, his face hidden behind a welding mask.

"Dale?"

Nothing.

"Dale."

Still nothing.

"DALE!"

He lifts the visor of his welding mask, which is funny because he's not welding anything, just doing some wiring work with a dinky little soldering iron.

"Jake, my young dude, meet Basszilla." His voice is husky with emotion. "With this bass, it will be possible to conquer the world."

"Or at least play some really low notes."

"*Really* low," he agrees. "Have a listen." He plugs the bass into an amp and hits a string. A powerful *BOOOOW-WWOOOOOOM* rattles the tools on Dale's workbench. He hits the next-lowest string. Every guitar in the shop sings. And under my shirt, my belly ripples like a pond when you drop a big rock in it.

It's not the Hum, exactly, but it's close.

"You okay?" Dale says. "You look a little sick."

"I'm just under a lot of stress."

"Oh, yeah? Still?" Dale mercifully mutes the resonating bass string with his palm and switches off the amp.

"I got grounded."

Dale nods. "I heard. Your mom was pretty vague on what you did."

"It wasn't my fault."

"Well, then getting grounded is an injustice. But you're not alone, dude. Life is a prison. We're all grounded. But this," he says, thumping my guitar bag with his finger, "this is the file in the cake."

As usual, I have no idea what Dale is saying when he's not talking about music.

"Your guitar, dude. It lets you saw through the jail cell bars. The guitar is your escape. And when you play with all your heart, you help everyone who listens escape their own prisons. It's not just a musical instrument. It's freedom."

I could use some freedom.

Freedom from being grounded (or "restricted," which my parents think sounds less like punishment). Freedom from the fear that people will discover my secret. Freedom from not having control over my own body.

I have a dangerous idea.

"Hey, Dale, could I play Basszilla?"

As soon as the words escape my lips, I have regrets. I want him to say no. But Dale doesn't say no to many things.

"Aw, yeah, my first guinea pig!"

Moments later, I'm on a stool with Basszilla over my knee and a giant amp thrumming behind me.

I start small, volume dialed low, lightly plucking the thinnest strings high up the neck. I do a couple of walking blues lines.

"Pay attention to your timing," Dale coaches. "Remember, the spaces between the notes are as important as the notes themselves."

I repeat the lines with a little more groove.

"That's it."

I go down the neck a little for lower notes, keeping the rhythm. When I'm comfortable, I dive a little lower, going for some runs on the thicker strings.

It sounds good and I'm doing okay, but I'm just playing stuff I could play on any bass. This isn't what Basszilla was designed for. It's not the kind of practice I need.

High up the neck again, I try some lines using the big seventh and eighth strings. And then, the ninth.

Now I'm feeling it in my guts—that deep, menacing, Hum-like throb.

"That was good, dude, but why'd you stop?"

"Just . . . getting used to the sound."

Again, I play the ninth string, thumping it with my thumb. Softly at first. Then a little less softly. Then I give it a good whack. The floor vibrates under my feet, and my middle feels a little swimmy. But as the note fades, I start to feel solid again. Good and solid.

"You've created a monster, Dale."

He grins, proud.

Maybe it's a monster I can get used to.

# CHAPTER 10

**"I GOT YOU SOMETHING!" AGNES** hands me a book as thick as a paving stone as we're walking out the school gates at the end of the day.

I read the title: *Physiology of Animal Species, A Zoological Compendium*.

"Aw, thanks, Agnes! A textbook! Just what I always wanted!"

"Did you get me anything?"

"No. I am a huge jerk. So what's the deal with the book?"

She drops to a whisper. "If you're going to be turning into things, you should develop a broad working knowledge of the animal kingdom. That way you'll have more options."

"Thank you. That's actually very thoughtful. But I don't think reading a chapter about"—I flip to the table of contents—"fiddle crickets is going to help me turn into a fiddle cricket on demand."

She nods like she can't wait for me to stop talking. "I know, that's why I built you this."

She passes me a metal box the size of a pack of American cheese. It has a single red knob that should probably be labeled *EXTREME DANGER*.

"What is this?"

"It's a frequency modulator with bass enhancer. Hook it up to your TV, turn the knob all the way to the right, and think of whatever animal you want. Bird, snake, dog— it doesn't matter. Well, probably don't think about fish. Unless you're in the tub. How far do the cables on your TV reach? Can you get the TV in the bathroom?"

We're still on school grounds, and anyone could easily mistake the box for a bomb. I try to give it back, but she won't take it.

"As soon as you told me about Basszilla I studied up on

audiology. That's the science of sound. I call the device the Hum-o-Tron. Plug the Hum-o-Tron into any good pair of speakers and it should give you low frequencies and high volume to simulate the Hum." She drops to an even lower whisper. "That way you can train yourself to master shape-shifting. I didn't have time to test it. To be honest, it could blow up your TV. And maybe rupture your eardrums. Do you have eardrums?"

"Yes, I have eardrums. And I don't want to practice . . . that thing you want me to practice. I want to practice *not* doing that thing. Can your box help me with that?"

Agnes's face changes. Not in an alien shapeshifting kind of way, but in a human, emotional kind of way. She's angry. "If you can learn to . . . do that thing, it would be a crime to not do that thing. You could be as strong as you want. As fast as you want. You could learn to fly like an owl. You could run like a cheetah. You could go anywhere, survive anywhere. You could save lives. And you don't even want to risk trying?"

"I know you want to help, Agnes. But what if I turn myself into an elephant and then can't turn back? Or what if I try to make myself a cricket only I end up like a giant kaiju? It's just too dangerous. Okay?"

I thrust the box back at her.

She takes it back. It's not okay.

"Agnes, come on . . ."

"I need to check up on the Fosters before martial arts lessons," she says. She turns her back to me and hurries off. Not until she's out of sight do I think about what kind of animal could have been strong enough to prevent boxes from crushing a forklift driver.

When I get home from school, Growler is on her belly, facing my closet, growling with her sharp little teeth bared. I don't think too much of it. Growler doesn't need a special reason to growl. Me playing guitar is enough. Or coughing. Or standing. Or existing.

But then someone inside the closet says, "This is a clever raincoat."

My mouth goes dry.

The smart thing to do in a situation like this is creep out of my room and call the police and tell my parents and maybe get out of the house.

Instead, I reach for the only weapon I have: my guitar.

Grasping the neck, I carry Stringy like a club and advance to the closet. I hope I don't have to hit anyone with it. I love Stringy.

I plant my feet and swing the closet door open.

It's the twins, Dairy and Gravy.

Gravy is wearing one of my flannel shirts over his head with the sleeves tied under his chin.

"Hello, Jake," says Gravy. "Greetings from your fellow bloblets."

"What are you doing here? I'm gonna call the cops."

There's no actual way I'm going to call the cops, because even if the twins are a new *they*, that doesn't mean the cops aren't still an old *they*.

"Be calm, sibling bloblet," says Dairy. "We are here to help."

"How did you even get up here?"

"We formed into insects and your wall mouth let us in." Dairy points at the window.

"You . . . you can turn into insects?"

"Of course," says Gravy. "We are like you. Only better at it. But we can help you."

I try to speak, but an avalanche of words gets stuck in my throat.

If they're telling the truth, that means the twins are like me.

That means I'm not the only shapeshifter, maybe not the only alien.

That means I'm not alone.

"Help me how?"

"You are too much like congealed grease, sibling bloblet. Like a hard, cold donut. You must learn to be hot grease. Only then can you be the kind of grease you wish to be."

"That made no sense. Not even a little. And why do you keep calling me bloblet?"

"Words are stiff. We are all bloblets from the same blob. We are like brothers and sister."

I have so many questions. Did they come from the same planet I did? Why do they know so much about what they are when I hardly know anything about myself?

But the question that spills from my mouth is "*Can* you teach me how to shapeshift?"

"Teaching? No. There is no teaching of us to you. But learning? Yes. You can learn to be yourself. And we can help you with that."

So, here I am with strangers in my closet with strangers

who know what I am because we're the same kind of weird. The tornado of thoughts swirling in my head makes me dizzy.

"How do I start?"

"This closet is confining," Dairy says. "Your house is confining. School is confining. But we have a place that is open."

Gravy nods. "You must come with us to our open place. It is way out in the desert."

"Like, a military complex with gleaming steel dissection tools? No, thanks."

"There are no gleaming steel dissection tools, bloblet. Do we appear dissected to you?"

They do not appear dissected, I have to admit. "Whatever, I can't go out in the desert with you."

"It is not *that* far," Dairy says. "It's at the dead mall. We will take you there after school."

The dead mall is only a few miles from here.

It's also where Agnes's tracker lost the hazmat creeps.

The Hum.

The sinkholes.

The xenogel.

The hazmat creeps.

My uncontrollable shifting.

And now, the twins, all connected like beads on a string.

Only it's a knotted string that I can't figure out how to untangle.

I'm dying to call Agnes right now.

"Monday," I say. "I can go with you after school on Monday."

That's only a couple of days away. And it's the only time when I'm not at school or under my parents' watchful eyes.

Dairy grins. I don't think she spends much time practicing normal smiles in the mirror, because her smile is pretty much ear to ear.

"This is a wonderful development! We will leave you to your strange and cramped quarters, then."

"Hey, wait. One more thing. How did you find me? How did you figure I'm . . . I'm like you?"

"Your friend," Gravy says, as though it's an insignificant question. "The girl. She led us to you."

My body goes stiff as beef jerky. My heart feels like it's tunneling to my knees. "You mean . . . Agnes?"

"Yes, the one called Agnes. You have no other friends. Except for us now. Until Monday. Then we will show you more blob."

Dairy and Gravy splash to the floor like a bucket of water after the bucket disappears.

One blink of the eye later, and they're a pair of houseflies.

They buzz past my ears and flit across the room. Growler does her best to catch them, and their high-pitched whines sound like laughter as they zip out the window and leave me alone with my racing brain.

# CHAPTER 11

**"YOU TOLD MY SECRET,"** I text to Agnes.

I wait a long time, expecting paragraphs telling me she didn't do it, didn't expose my secret. Or pages of explanations, telling me why she did it.

But all she sends back is, "I'm sorry. Can we talk?"

So that's it, then.

She told Dairy and Gravy about me.

I turn off my phone and leave it off all through the long, sad weekend.

At school on Monday, I refuse to look at her.

"Jake . . ." she says in Advisory.

I don't answer.

She tries to pass me a note.

I don't read it.

I spend lunch in the library, instead of with Agnes.

When school lets out, she tries one more time.

"Please talk to me," she pleads outside the gate.

Her voice shakes and her eyes are moist. There's nothing Night Kite about her now. She's hardly even recognizable as Agnes, and I feel awful for brushing past her, over to the curb where my mom is waiting in the car.

She's the one who should feel awful. She was my only friend. And she gave away my biggest secret.

Mom's in a talky mood as she drives me to my guitar lesson. I figure talking is why she's taking me instead of Dad.

"Your dad and I understand why you didn't tell us you shifted into a seal at the mall. We shouldn't have held the prospect of home school like a sword hanging over your neck."

I shrug. "My neck can get pretty rubbery. A sword wouldn't be that bad."

"Hm. So you wouldn't mind home school?"

"I didn't say that. What if I never learn how to control my shifting? Are you going to homeschool me until I graduate high school? And then online college? And then some kind of job I can do without ever leaving the house?"

"A lot of kids are homeschooled. A lot of people do college remotely. And a lot of people work at home."

"It's not the same thing, Mom."

She releases a puff of air. "No, it's not. We never wanted home to be a prison. We're your parents and we love you. We want you to be whatever you want to be and soar as high as you can." She thinks about what she just said. "But no birds in the house. I will not tolerate poop in my kitchen."

I laugh. Just a little bit. It feels like I haven't laughed in a long time.

"Your dad and I don't always know how to help you be the most Jake you can be while keeping you safe. We're just trying to figure this stuff out as we go along. And we're going to make mistakes."

"I guess there aren't a lot of how-to-parent-an-alien books in the library."

"There aren't, and believe me, we've looked. But one thing is certain. You're not a problem. You're our son. And you're not special because you can change shape. You're special because you're kind. Because you're funny. Because you take great care of Growler. You're our Jake who plays guitar and dreams of doing something special with his talent. The one who climbs up on the roof and strums in the night."

The conversation had been going so well.

"You know about that?"

Mom laughs. "We can hear Growler growling at you, even with the windows shut and the AC on."

"You never told me to stop. You don't mind?"

"We're terrified that you'll fall. But we don't want to keep you chained down. Do you understand?"

I do understand.

But there are things *they* don't understand.

It's not just that I don't know where I'm from. It's not just that I'm out of control. It's that I don't even know what I am.

It's time for me to get answers, even though it means lying to Mom and Dad again.

Mom goes across the street to work at the coffee shop, and I dive into Dale's. Dale is behind the counter, putting strings on an electric. He holds it up for me to see. "Fender Telecaster. Look at that sunburst finish. Not a scratch on 'er. What do you think?"

I think it's beautiful and I want to plug into a giant

amplifier and strum my heart out, but I don't have time for that.

I hand him Stringy. "I think there's something wrong with the neck. I'm getting a buzz on the seventh fret. Can you have a look?"

We go into the back room, and Dale lays Stringy on the worktable, right next to Basszilla. Within seconds, he's completely absorbed in his work, and he doesn't even look up as I slip out the back door, into the alley behind the store.

A van waits for me there, the engine running. It is white. And unmarked.

A man and a woman sit in the front seat. They're dressed in regular clothes. The man is at the wheel. The woman is chewing on a burrito, spaghetti spilling from the tortilla. They're the hazmat creeps from the Fosters' house.

They tell me their names are Leonard and Tami as the side door opens, revealing the twins.

I should absolutely, under no circumstances, get in the van with them.

I get in the van with them.


The van stops in the nearly empty parking lot behind Cactus Center, otherwise known as the dead mall. To be fair, it's not *entirely* dead. Just mostly. There're still a few random shops open, plus the Tumbleweed Diner, where only retired people eat. And I'm sure a lot of creepy mannequins hang out in the dark, shuttered stores.

It took us nine minutes to get here, so if it takes the same amount of time to get back to Dale's, that leaves me forty-two minutes to learn everything I want to know about myself and about shapeshifting.

I climb out and follow Tami and Leonard and the twins to the entrance of what used to be a department store. The windows are painted over in black, and above, on the building's face, ghostly white letters and bolt holes are all that remain of the store's sign. Mounted next to the glass doors is a sleek, black security system thing. Tami presses some numbers on a keypad, covering her hand with the other one so I can't see her code. She removes her sunglasses, opens her right eye wide, and leans into a little camera lens. There's a buzz and some clicks, and she pushes the door open.

The security stuff is a bit unsettling, but it's also kind of cool.

Inside, it's less cool, just a big space with some torn-up carpet, crowded with bare clothes racks and mirrors and glass cases with nothing in them.

And, yep, there are mannequins. A lot of them: plastic, naked, most missing heads and limbs, and a few of them wearing wigs that look like bad taxidermy.

"Do the fake plastic people please you?" asks Gravy. "There are many more in the dark basement where they exist by themselves amidst the skittering of small rodents."

"There are also ghostly moans," says Dairy. "They are caused by old air-conditioning equipment. Probably. We can take you down there if you wish."

"Thanks, but I'm kind of on a tight schedule." I tap my wrist as if I'm wearing a watch.

"The good stuff's upstairs," says Leonard. He and Tami lead us up a squeaking escalator.

At the top, I step onto a gleaming white floor and find myself in a completely different world. A vast space bustles with people, some in business suits, some in lab coats, a few in hazmat suits. Rows of work desks and computers stretch into the distance. Big screens mounted on the walls display graphs and numbers and stuff that maybe even Agnes wouldn't understand.

This is more like the high-tech science-y stuff I was expecting.

A woman with neat hair and neat clothes and a neat face approaches. I recognize her. "I'm Dr. Woll," she says, offering a handshake.

Dr. Woll. The person who came by our house on the first day of school asking questions about sinkholes.

This means she's connected to the twins.

And to the hazmat creeps.

And to the imblobsters who replaced the Fosters.

None of which she mentioned to my parents at the door.

I don't return her handshake, even though that's impolite. I can't trust her.

"I've told people where I'm going and if you try to dissect me or something, they will know about it. So don't do anything bad or weird."

I haven't told anyone where I'm going, and Woll could totally dissect me and no one would ever know.

Woll smiles and raises a hand. "I solemnly promise that I will not dissect you, nor do anything bad or weird. Now, I know we're short on time today, and I want you to get as much from this visit as possible, so shall we get started? Davy, Mary, why don't you go eat some candy?"

"Dr. Woll is our monkey," Gravy confides. He and

Dairy agreeably head off somewhere.

"Do they ever make sense?"

"Not recently," Woll says, with a shadow of sadness.

She leads me down a corridor lined with workers hunched over computers and microscopes and flasks and bottles. As we walk, people come up to her with tablets and clipboards, some of which she looks at, some of which she signs, some of which she waves away.

"We're a partnership of business, government, and military," Woll tells me. "A collaboration. And our mission is very specialized research. So, collaboration plus laboratory equals . . . ?"

"Collaboratory?"

She snaps her fingers. "You got it, Jake."

Stopping in front of a computer screen, she clicks a mouse. Up comes a familiar image: a map of Cedar Creek View.

"Twelve years ago, a mass of xenogel fell to Earth. But you know that. Xenogel is a metamorphic compound with extraterrestrial origins." She clicks the mouse again. Several red dots appear on the map. It only takes me a few seconds to realize what they're marking. Cedar Creek View Middle School. The Fosters' house. The Cedar Creek View Fashion

Valley Galleria Mall. Half a dozen other locations.

"Sinkholes," I say.

She gives me a nod and a pleasant smile. "And at every one of the sinkhole sites, we've found this." She takes a little glass cylinder sealed with a black rubber stopper from her pocket. A few drops of silvery gray fluid wiggle inside.

"We call it xenogel, and it's spreading under Cedar Creek View. Expanding. Reproducing. It's reaching out, for what purpose, we don't know. How far it will spread, we have no idea. Does it have a plan? We haven't got a clue."

She pauses, maybe thinking I need time to process this information. But all I can think is, I'm xenogel, the same as the stuff underground, reproducing.

"Can you show me how to stop changing shape when I don't want to?"

"Absolutely. And so much more than that."

"I'll be able to turn into any animal?"

Woll laughs. "Jake, that's just the beginning. You're capable of so much more. We can help you achieve your full potential."

Part of me says, Yes, cooperate with them. You deserve answers and knowledge.

It's everything I want.

Another part of me says, Remember the Fosters.

Here I am, taking a tour of a science lab, hoping to get something out of it, like I'm the only important person in this whole thing. If Agnes were here, finding out what happened to the Fosters would be her priority. And she wouldn't be shy about it. Night Kite is not shy. She'd just come right out and demand answers.

"So, what happened to the Foster family? Are they dead?"

Woll smiles. I can usually tell the difference between a nervous smile, a truly friendly smile, and a fake smile.

I can't tell anything at all from Dr. Woll's smile.

"The Fosters?" she says. "You know them?"

"I was there when they got taken over by the xenogel blob. I saw what happened to them."

"You keep late hours, Jake. Tell me, what did you see?"

"There was a sinkhole. Xenogel came out of the sinkhole. It gobbed over all three Fosters, and then the Fosters were . . ."

"Were what?"

"They were all . . . weird. They talked funny. They didn't know how kitchens work."

"So, not dead, then."

"No, maybe not, but imblobstered."

"Blob plus imposter. I like that." Woll smiles again. This time it looks like a genuine smile. "Well, Jake, as you said, the Fosters are at home, right where they're supposed to be. As for them behaving weirdly, it's no surprise that coming into contact with the xenogel left them disoriented. There's still so much we don't know about how the xenogel works. For example, the xenogel did something to the Fosters, but I assume you can touch people and objects without 'imblobstering' them?"

I have to hand it to her. That's a very good question. When I was a baby blob, my dad touched me, and I didn't imblobster him. I just became a human baby. And I've touched millions of things ever since.

Woll looks at her watch. "Few things get done in a single afternoon, and I hope this won't be your only visit. In any case, it's getting late, and I don't want you to leave here today without gaining something of value. So why don't we show you what you really are?"

My heart thuds. I swallow. "Yes. Yes, I would like that."

On our way down a corridor, a worker hands her a small tablet. "You left this in the cafeteria, Doctor."

"We've been busy here," Woll explains to me. "I'm losing track of things."

The picture on the lock screen is Woll and two kids. Blond. Blue-eyed. A boy and a girl. It's the twins, Dairy and Gravy. They're smiling nice, happy, smiles. Even though they're identical to Gravy and Dairy, they're somehow . . . different. More normal.

Dr. Woll takes me into a white-walled lab dominated by a cylindrical tank in the center of the room. The tank is about the size of a refrigerator. Liquid swirls inside, the same vivid blue as toilet bowl cleaner. Maybe it is toilet bowl cleaner. Maybe this is a giant toilet. I don't know science stuff.

She taps the screen of her tablet a few times. From the top of the tank descends a thumb-sized blob of silvery-gray goo.

"Xenogel?" I ask.

"An isolated strand of it. We took it from the sinkhole at 33 degrees, 27 minutes, 47 seconds north, 112 degrees, 23 minutes, 46 seconds west."

"Those sure were a lot of numbers and words."

"Sorry. We like to be precise here. That's the parking

lot outside the Cedar Creek View Fashion Valley Galleria Mall." She sets her tablet down on a desk. "Have you heard of the Humongous Fungus?"

I bet Agnes has heard of the Humongous Fungus. Agnes, whom Woll hasn't mentioned once, even though it was Agnes who betrayed me and told Gravy and Dairy what I was.

"No."

"Its proper name is *Armillaria ostoyae*, and it's the largest living being on Earth, a fungal organism that covers almost four square miles of the Malheur National Forest. We think the xenogel beneath Cedar Creek View is like that, only possibly bigger."

"Then . . . I'm part of a bigger living being?"

Woll checks her watch again. "We have thirteen minutes to get you back to your mother. I'll call for Tami and Leonard."

She sets her tablet down and digs her phone out of her pocket.

I can't help wondering how much Agnes could find on that tablet.

While Woll's distracted calling for my ride home, I reach for it.

Unlike Agnes, I don't carry around a backpack, and I don't even have a pocket big enough to stash it in. But I do have something almost nobody else does: the ability to make my own pocket. The twins can change shape without being shaken and stirred and softened by the Hum, and if they can do it, why can't I?

Be like hot grease, they told me. Be less congealed.

Or maybe, to say it in a less weird way, I just have to relax. Loosen up. This shouldn't be much more complicated than forking my tongue or giving myself webbed toes.

While Woll's on the phone, I close my eyes and picture soft, loose things. Melting ice cream. A can of soup plopping in a kettle. Pudding.

In one quick motion, I snatch the tablet and tuck it under my shirt, and dunk it into my pudding belly. It goes in with a little burping noise. Now it's inside me.

It's gross.

I'm gross.

But I have the tablet.

# CHAPTER 12

**MY STOMACH RUMBLES WITH WOLL'S** tablet inside. I talk to the twins to cover the noise. We're in the back of the van with Tami and Leonard in the front.

"When you said Woll was your monkey, that's not really what you meant, is it?"

"She is definitely our monkey," Gravy says. "And we love her very much."

"Do you mean mother?"

"Bake is correct," says Dairy. "Woll is our beloved mother."

I don't even bother to correct her about my name.

"Does that mean she's also a goo alien? Does that mean . . ." I have a hard time actually getting the words out. "Does that mean, she's my mother, too?"

Dairy laughs. "No, Bake. You are funny."

The van finally pulls into the alley behind Dale's.

Tami unlocks the door. "We'll be in touch about your next visit."

"Okay, good, great," I say, getting out.

Dashing through the back door of the guitar shop, I wave at a confused and befuddled Dale, who's still absorbed in diagnosing Stringy's neck, and I make a straight line out the front door.

Mom stands down the street beside our parked car. And with her is Agnes on her bike.

I stroll up casually. Am I overdoing it? Should I have aimed for jaunty instead of casual?

"Hi?" I say.

"Hey, Jake," Mom says. "Where's your guitar?"

"I left it with Dale. There's a buzz on the seventh fret."

That sounded normal. I think.

"I was just telling your mom how I wanted to check out the guitar shop," says Agnes. She's out of breath, red-faced, sweating.

"You never told me Agnes plays guitar," Mom says, as if I've been keeping a secret.

"That is right. I never did tell you that."

Does Agnes play guitar? I don't think so. But she could probably learn it in a couple of hours while doing push-ups.

"Ms. Wind, I need to talk to Jake for a second." Agnes begins to walk off. When I don't follow, she pinches my shirtsleeve and leads me away.

At the corner, a little too close to Big Blue Biter the mailbox, she says, "The tracker I planted on the hazmat creeps went off and led me here. I tried to reach you, but your phone must be broken—"

"I turned it off." My voice drips with ice.

Her mouth hangs open. "Okay. Well, I raced here because I knew you had a guitar lesson, but by the time I got here, you were gone. And then the tracker said the van was heading back to the dead mall. I put two and two together, and . . . did they kidnap you? Are you okay? What did they do to you? How did you escape?"

"The twins visited me at home on Friday, and I went with them today voluntarily. I met Dr. Woll there. She knew who I was. She knew what I was. She knows all about me. And it's your fault."

Agnes closes her eyes. When she opens them, she looks at the sidewalk, at the mailbox, anywhere but at me. This, from a person whose stare is usually so direct it could burn holes in concrete. She takes a breath and holds it, like she dreads letting it out. Then, "I contacted Dr. Woll," she admits. "I told her about the goo sample we collected from the sinkhole on the first day of school."

My throat closes up. "You said you wouldn't."

"I know. I didn't think there'd be any harm in it." Her throat sounds a little closed up, too. "I used an anonymous email address to contact her, and I mailed her the sample without a return address. There shouldn't have been any way for her to identify me. There shouldn't have been any way for her to identify *you*."

"Well, thanks to you, she did."

"But how?"

I struggle to keep my voice down. "That doesn't even matter. You made a promise."

"I know you're upset, but the only reason we agreed to keep the investigation to ourselves was because it would be more fun that way. That's what you said. That's what I agreed to."

"You know I had more reasons than that to keep this a secret."

"I know that *now*. But I didn't until the seal incident.

And I sent Woll the goo sample *before* I knew you were an alien."

"So you've been lying to me for a while."

Red rises to Agnes's cheeks. "You were lying to me longer than that."

If I let my cheeks turn red, I'll probably become a full-on lobster, so I try to stay calm.

I glance over to Mom to make sure she's not watching, and then I reach under my shirt. There's a loud plopping pudding sound, but it's not difficult to expel the tablet from my belly, because my belly doesn't really want to keep holding it inside.

"Was that . . . in you?"

"Yeah," I say, embarrassed for some reason.

"That's weird but cool."

"Just take it."

She holds out a Ziploc bag and has me drop the tablet inside.

"Who does this belong to?"

"It's Woll's."

Her eyes get big.

"Jake?" Mom calls from down the street. "Time to get a move on."

"Be right there!" I lean in closer to Agnes. "Woll told me some stuff, but I think she's holding back. Do your Night Kite wizardry on the tablet and see if you can find anything out."

Agnes gives me a firm, businesslike nod.

As I turn to walk away, she says softly, "I'm sorry I sent Woll the goo sample."

I pretend I don't hear her and walk faster.

# CHAPTER 13

**BENEATH A SPRAY OF STARS** in the calm night sky, I sit cross-legged on the roof. The brightest of the stars glare at me like they're accusing me of something.

Growler, curled up in my lap, growls when I scritch behind her ears. I wish I had my guitar. My fingers are twitchy, but Stringy is still with Dale for the seventh-fret buzz I lied about. I should probably call him and tell him Stringy's fine.

Growler's growl changes pitch to a warning. I brace myself for . . . something.

Agnes's head appears over the edge of the roof. "I know I'm the last person you want to see right now, but can I come up?"

Growler settles back into a normal growl.

"Growler says okay."

"What do you say?"

"I don't know."

Agnes springs nimbly over the eaves and sits a couple of feet away from me, giving me space. The rumble of air conditioners fills the painful silence.

"Any news about the Fosters?" I ask after a while.

"Just came from there. Their car's still in the driveway, and the sinkhole's filled in. But they're not home."

"That's bad, right?"

"Probably, yeah."

The air conditioners rumble on.

I clear my throat. "I've been thinking, how did Woll know I was an alien just from the goo sample you sent her? How did she link it to me?"

"Good question. Have you figured it out?"

"The first day we saw the twins at school, they were collecting garbage and I gave them my juice carton. They must have brought it back to the Collaboratory along with all the other trash. Woll knew the goo from space splash-landed here twelve years ago, so there was a good chance that if any of the alien goo took human form, they might be attending Cedar Creek View Middle School. She probably ID'd me from traces I left on the carton."

"Yeah," was all Agnes said.

"That means it wasn't your fault. I shouldn't have accused you of betraying me. I'm sorry."

"And I shouldn't have sent her the sample. We agreed we wouldn't. So, I'm sorry."

Crickets chirp, invisible in the dark.

Agnes removes Woll's tablet from her backpack. "I've been working on this. Most of the files are encrypted. I haven't cracked them yet, but I did access a few files. Stuff that Woll probably didn't think was all that important. I found out some things, and I wanted to talk to you face-to-face." She hesitates. "It's bad news. Do you want to hear it?"

I do not want to hear it. But not hearing it won't make the news less bad. "Okay."

She taps in a password.

"How'd you figure out her password?"

"If you're going to be a crime-fighter, you must learn the methods and practices of criminals."

"Are you saying you did something wrong?"

Agnes scrolls through screens. "I did something illegal.

That doesn't mean it's wrong. It used to be illegal for women to vote. If thwarting evil is illegal, then I'd rather be a criminal. Anyway, you're the one who stole the tablet."

"I wonder if Woll's figured that out yet."

"She's not stupid. But I blocked her ability to track it or change the password."

She hands me the tablet. The screen shows a diagram made of white dots connected by white lines. It reminds me of a spiderweb flecked with dewdrops. The drops are all labeled with numbers.

"A star chart?"

"Yes." She taps the screen, and two of the dots change from white to green. So does the line connecting them. "This is our sun. And this is the Crab Nebula." From her backpack comes an enormous pair of binoculars. She points them at the sky and spends a few seconds looking and focusing. "There it is. Have a look."

I take the binoculars and aim where she's pointing.

"I don't see anything."

"A tiny bit left. A little more. Just a bit up. See the gray smudge?"

"Okay, I see it."

Agnes takes a breath. "That's where you're from."

I think I gasp a little.

"Jake . . ."

"Just give me a second, okay?"

I keep looking, imagining myself as a blob, sailing through all that empty space between the Crab Nebula and Earth. Did I have any thoughts back then? Things I've forgotten? Or was I just peacefully asleep for the whole journey, without a trouble on my mind?

I have to force myself to lower the binoculars and come back down to Earth.

"What's the bad news?"

"The Crab Nebula is sixty-five hundred light-years away. That means the light leaving it takes sixty-five hundred years to reach our eyes here on Earth."

My brain churns. "If I came from there . . . then I spent at least sixty-five hundred years in space. That means I'm older than the pyramids in Egypt. It means I'm older than—"

"The English language," Agnes says softly. "Older than Stonehenge. Older than the invention of the chicken."

"But I don't have any memories from before I landed

here. I don't feel that old. This doesn't feel like bad news."

Usually Agnes can't wait to tell me things. Not this time. This time, it's like she has to tear it out of herself.

"The nebula is a supernova remnant," she says. "A supernova remnant is the remains of a dead star. That means . . . it means . . ."

Oh.

I get it now.

"The star doesn't exist anymore. It's gone. The place I'm from . . . my planet . . . my home . . . is gone."

Agnes looks like she's in actual physical pain. "Yes, Jake."

I can't find a word to describe how I feel. It's not like I ever knew my home world. If it still existed, if it hadn't burned up in the fire of an exploding star thousands of years ago, it's not like I could hop into a spaceship and go there now. So why should I feel bad about any of this? Why should I feel so hollow inside? Why should I feel so lost?

I wipe my eyes. "That sucks."

Agnes lets me sniffle in silence. She doesn't try to tell me I shouldn't be sad. She doesn't try to cheer me up. She just lets me be alone while keeping me company.

"We're still friends?" I say eventually.

She gives me a light punch on the shoulder. "Friends and allies. Night Kite and Star Hammer."

"More like Night Kite and Star Pudding."

We laugh.

I feel just a tiny little bit better.

# CHAPTER 14

**WHILE I WRESTLE WITH THE** idea of being an ancient orphan from a dead world, and while alien goo expands beneath the surface of Cedar Creek View, I still have to go to class.

"Writing on paper is a normal school activity!" says Mr. Brown with more cheer than I've ever heard from him. "Everyone! Get out paper and write on it."

The entire class blinks and stares at him.

Parker Zeballos raises her hand. "What are we supposed to write about?"

"Appropriate school things!" Mr. Brown says with alarming enthusiasm. "I will engage in this activity as well."

He scribbles away.

"What the ever heck?" I whisper to Agnes.

"I'm going to conduct an experiment on him," she whispers back.

She gets out a blank piece of paper and brings it up to Mr. Brown's desk. "I've completed my appropriate school writing."

Mr. Brown beams at her. "You are very good at school writing."

And now, Agnes does something incredible. She removes a little package from her pocket. And from the package she withdraws a foil-wrapped strip.

It's gum.

The room grows quiet as we all watch this drama play out. Every crinkle of the foil sounds like a car crash. When she puts the gum in her mouth and works her jaw, I can hear how it sticks and pulls away from her teeth. I can hear her sloshing saliva. We all can. Agnes is chewing gum, right in Mr. Brown's face. And not just chewing it. She's smacking it. She's massacring it.

"Is that gum?" asks Mr. Brown.

We tense for an explosion.

"Yes," Agnes says between the horrible grinding

motions of the entire lower half of her face. "It's chewing gum. And I am chewing it."

"What an interesting activity," says Mr. Brown. "I, too, would like to chew gum."

She hands Mr. Brown a piece. He unwraps it. He puts it between his teeth and sucks it in like a vending machine taking a dollar.

Mr. Brown is chewing gum in class.

Something's happened to the real Mr. Brown. He's been replaced, just like the Foster family.

He's an imblobster.

First the Fosters.

And now Mr. Brown.

I take a look around the room.

If Mr. Brown's an imblobster, anyone could be.

Anyone at school.

Anyone who was near the mall.

Anyone who was near any of the sinkholes.

Anyone.

Maybe it's odd that with everything going on I can still enjoy stale chicken nuggets on the edge of the soccer field, but Agnes is enjoying nothing, which sort of evens things out. She taps away at Woll's tablet, muttering words you're not supposed to say at school, such as "#%@$" and "%^&@$."

"Night Kite never curses," I remind her around a mouthful of stubborn nugget.

"$%^&@#@!" she says.

"Still can't get into those encrypted files?"

"I got into them fine."

I swallow some nugget. "Wow, really? When did that happen?"

"During breakfast push-ups. I took a free online encryption course last night, and it led to a breakthrough."

"That's fantastic, Agnes! So why are you saying '%^&@$'?"

"Because it's not like Woll's got a file named 'TOP_SECRET_PLAN_DO_NOT_READ.' It's just endless work stuff. Payroll. Employee schedules. Purchase orders."

"Jobs are boring," I observe.

"I mean, just listen to this stuff: Five thousand sticky note pads. Twenty cases of printer paper. Four gross cartons of toilet paper."

"Why would they buy gross toilet paper?"

"Gross is a quantity, Jake. It means twelve dozen."

"I just learned something!" I eat a nugget.

Agnes goes on listing all the things the Collaboratory has purchased, and after a while I understand why she's been cursing. It's a very long list.

"Fifteen miles of copper wire, speaker cones, capacitors, rectifier modules—"

"Wait. Those are things that Dale has lying around in his shop. They're amplifier parts."

"Dale's shop doesn't have room for the size of these components. We're talking twelve-foot-diameter speaker cones. Six of them."

I spit nugget bits. "Agnes, that's it! You found the answer. I know what the Collaboratory is doing. With an amplifier that big, you could make a huge noise. A huge, deep, low noise."

"A noise like . . . like a Hum. But why? What does the Collaboratory get out of it?"

"Think about what the Hum does."

"It turns you all pudding-y and shifts you into a seal."

"I think we're almost there, Agnes. We're really close to figuring this all out."

Agnes gets a determined look on her face. A Night Kite look. "There's only one thing to do, Jake."

"Don't say it."

"I am going to say it. We have to break into the Collaboratory and spy on them and then thwart their plan!"

"You're just looking for an excuse to crawl through air shafts and play with smoke bombs."

"Jake," she says, very seriously, "I'm going to share with you my philosophy of life, the one and only thing in the whole universe I know to be true. I think you're ready to hear this."

I check my pocket for a pen to write down whatever Agnes says next. "Okay. I'm ready."

"If you are ever given a chance to climb through air shafts and toss smoke bombs, *you absolutely must climb through air shafts and toss smoke bombs*."

"That definitely does sound like your philosophy. Me, my philosophy is *if you are ever given a chance to be dissected, you probably should avoid being dissected*."

"Ugh, Jake, that *is* a good philosophy," she says, deflated.

The bell chimes, and we get up to go to our classes.

"Let me think about it."

"Fair enough. I really don't want you to get dissected."

"I know. That's what makes us friends."

Agnes heads off to Geometry, and I'm on my way to Math for People Who Aren't as Smart as Agnes when Dairy and Gravy catch me alone.

"Bloblet Jake," Dairy calls out.

I have no idea if they even attend class or just hang out on campus as insects or erasers until they want to bother me.

"Will you be regurgitating to the Collaboratory?" asks Gravy.

"I hope you mean 'returning' to the Collaboratory."

"Which is the one that means coming up from the stomach and spilling all over the place?"

"That's regurgitating."

"Please do not do that at the Collaboratory. Please do the other thing."

"I . . . I don't know."

Dairy blinks. Gravy blinks, too. They blink at the exact same time. Maybe it's an imblobster thing. Maybe it's just a twin thing.

"But don't you wish to be less congealed so you can turn into bugs and sledgehammers whenever you want?" says Gravy.

"You guys can turn into sledgehammers?"

"Sledgehammers are easy, Cake. They don't even have moving parts. So, tell us, when can you regurgitate and be a sledgehammer?"

I almost agree to it. I could ditch school and we could go right now and after a few lessons maybe I could stop worrying about bird hands and mall seals. And I could discover exactly what Woll's up to. I'm being offered a free ride to the house of secrets.

But maybe it'd only be a one-way ride. I still don't know what the Collaboratory wants with me. But I know they kept the news about the death of my home planet from me.

"I don't think I can come back," I tell the twins.

They cock their heads to the side like confused dogs.

"Words are stiff," Dairy says. "Maybe we misunderstood."

"No, you didn't. I can't come back. You talk about helping me, but Dr. Woll—"

"—our monkey," Gravy interrupts.

"I can't trust your monkey. So I'm not going to regurgitate to the Collaboratory. I should never have gone in the first place."

Dairy smiles, not quite an ear-to-ear grin, but close enough. "What is the name of your noisy beast?"

The question comes from out of the blue.

"My dog?"

"Is your dog the hairy one that hates many things?"

"Her name is Growler. And she doesn't hate me."

"Growler," Dairy says.

"Growler," Gravy agrees.

Dairy winks. "See you soon, Cake."

After dinner I step onto the window ledge with Growler in the crook of my arm. Up the paloverde tree, steady on the rain gutter, and onto the roof I go.

Streetlights mark the boundaries of Cedar Creek View. In the darkness on the edge of town lurks the dead mall. My eyes lift from street level to the night sky. I can't see the Crab Nebula without Agnes's binoculars, but I know where it is now. Ever since Agnes told me my home planet was gone, burned to a crisp by an exploding star thousands of years ago, I haven't stopped looking up.

With my face pressed into Growler's pungent scruff, I watch the silent stars twinkle.

Something occurs to me. Growler has not growled. Not since I got home from school. Not while I hauled her up to the roof. Not a single time.

"Are you sick, girl?"

She looks at me but doesn't growl.

Maybe she's got a stomachache. I gently prod her tummy. She doesn't flinch. She doesn't make a noise.

One by one, I take each of her legs and extend them to see if she's in pain. I inspect her paws and rub a finger over the pads.

No reaction.

No growl.

She looks like Growler.

She feels like Growler.

But I know my dog.

This is not Growler.

# CHAPTER 15

**THE TWINS IMBLOBSTERED MY DOG.** They practically told me they were going to do it.

Okay.

If they want me back at the Collaboratory so bad, they're going to get what they wish for.

I'm going to shift into a sledgehammer and break down their doors.

I'm going to shift into a bulldozer and smash through their walls.

I'm going to crush anyone who gets in my way.

Nobody messes with my dog.

Agnes spends about two hundred minutes on the phone trying to talk me out of it.

The only thing that makes me listen to her is *Star Hammer* Annual #6.

"Remember what happened when Professor Brainpan abducted Nails the Star Horse?"

I do remember. It was a trap, and Brainpan imprisoned Star Hammer in a subatomic condenser field.

"And all Woll needs to trap you is a bucket with a tight lid."

Agnes is right, and I hate it.

"We'll make them turn Growler back to normal tomorrow," she promises. "Try to sleep. I have a feeling tomorrow's going to be a big action scene."

I spend most of the night on the roof, glaring toward the dead mall. I don't have my guitar. I don't have my dog. The only thing that keeps me company is my worry and rage.


Agnes and I meet before class the next day. She has a plan. It's pretty simple. We're going to ditch school.

We walk right up to the chain link fence bordering the administration offices. Agnes points in the opposite direction and hollers, "OH MY GOD IS THAT A DEAD BODY?"

While everyone's distracted trying to spot a corpse,

we scramble over the fence and run away to the little park three blocks from school. There's no one here but us, a couple of people doing yoga on the grass, and a couple of dads pushing a little kid on the swings. It's a very pleasant scene.

I don't like it.

"Any of them could be an imblobster," I warn Agnes as she leads us to some bushes. "Anyone anywhere could be an imblobster."

Behind the bushes lie a pair of bikes. There's Agnes's and . . .

"That's my bike. You stole my bike?"

"I relocated it for your convenience."

"It was in the garage. And locked."

"I know. You didn't make it easy on me, thanks very much."

"I apologize that I didn't make it easier to steal my bike?"

"I forgive you. C'mon, it's a long ride to the dead mall."

From our surveillance point across the street, the mall looks harmless. Elderly people go in and out of the Tumbleweed Diner. A few people head into the mall itself. But overall, the dead mall is dead.

Agnes goes over the infiltration plan with me.

Unlike ditching school, it's complicated. It involves me doing things I'm not sure I can do. It involves air shafts. It involves rope. It's a whole heist.

"There," she says, watching a van exit the parking lot. It's white and unmarked.

"Is it Tami and Leonard?"

"It's their van, at least."

She takes a little metal box with a red knob from her backpack: the Hum-o-Tron. I refused it the first time she tried to give it to me, but this time I take it, along with a clunky pair of modified headphones. This is going to be the hardest shift I've ever done on purpose, and I need help.

"Are you sure you want to do this?" she asks.

"Absolutely."

"You don't have to. I don't want you to do something you don't want to do. I can find us another way."

"Thanks, Agnes. That means a lot to me. But it's a good plan."

"Okay, then."

She affixes the headphones over my ears. They're a bit crampy. Next, she plugs the headphones into the box and then turns the red knob a little.

I hear a bit of Hum and give her a thumbs-up.

She turns the knob a little more.

Gradually, a deep vibration fills my head. The roots of my teeth ache. The little fleshy punching bag in the back of my throat shivers.

I take a deep breath and give her another thumbs-up.

She turns the knob some more.

Now it feels like a real Hum. Like I'm a tuning fork. Like I contain earthquakes. My bones scream with a searing ache.

I let the Hum travel through me and stop thinking of my body as a mass of solid matter but instead as specks of material—hair, skin, muscle, bone. The specks have to loosen, become as liquid as my blood. Less like ice. More like water.

The pain starts to fade. I feel like I'm letting out a long-held breath.

Muscles form beneath my surface.

My bones stretch.

My insides move and change.

My hair lengthens.

Calluses form on my knuckles.

Some parts shrink. Other parts swell.

Standing tall, I look down at Agnes.

"Did I do it?" My voice is different. Lower. I don't sound like me.

Agnes doesn't say anything.

"Did I mess it up? Do I have a parrot mouth? Tell me!" I feel my face. I don't detect a beak.

"You shifted perfectly," Agnes says finally. "You're amazing."

I do feel pretty amazing, I have to admit.

"Well, your box helped."

"It's true. I am also amazing. Do you remember the plan? And the backup plan? And the backup to the backup plan? Maybe I should come up with a backup to the backup to the backup plan."

"That would be too many plans. I'd forget some of them."

There's nothing left to do, so I set off to the crosswalk.

"Hey," Agnes calls after me. "You can count on me."

I turn and smile at her with Tami's mouth.

Once I'm at the department store entrance, I punch in the password Agnes got from Woll's tablet. I'm not gassed or electrocuted or mobbed by security guards, so I guess step one of the plan is going okay.

I lean toward the camera with my right eye open wide.

"Retinal scan fail," says a fuzzy voice from a speaker somewhere. "Try again."

"I think it's broken," I say.

"Everything seems to be working from here."

"Obviously not, or I'd be on my way to the break room right now to microwave my burrito."

I hold a wrapped burrito up to the camera. It's a butterscotch burrito for authenticity. Another thing Agnes thought of.

"Okay, sorry, Tami."

The lock buzzes. I step into the dark space with the empty clothes racks and creepy naked mannequins. The escalator delivers me into bright light and clacking computer keys. A few people walk past me without looking up. Someone says, "Hi, Tami," but keeps on going.

I've done it. I'm in the Collaboratory.

This was the easy part.

I don't know where to begin, so I just start wandering, poking my head into rooms, peeking into windowed offices, looking for something, *anything*, that will help me return my dog to her regular, obnoxious self instead of the silent thing I left locked in the bathroom (with food and water and air-conditioning because I'm not a monster).

People seem more stressed and hurried than the other time I was here, like they're under some kind of deadline.

I slip through a big green door marked *Xenomorphic Tank*. Inside is a massive steel structure resembling a cross between a bathtub and a submarine. It's studded with valves and dials and little round porthole windows. I recognize the substance swirling slowly inside. It's xenogel.

Workers in hazmat suits crawl around, checking and adjusting controls. One of them wheels up a big vacuum-cleaner thing connected to a clear plastic barrel full of xenogel. He connects a hose to the big tank and flips a switch. The vacuum-cleaner thing rumbles and the barrel empties.

Another worker drives a beeping forklift up to the tank. Resting on the forks is a blue mailbox. I notice the scratches and dents, and I realize it's not just any mailbox, but the one down the corner from Dale's.

It's Big Blue Biter.

The forklift raises Big Blue Biter to the top of the tank and dumps it in through a hatch. The mailbox sinks through the gel, blurring and softening and turning into fluid. Within seconds, there's no Big Blue Biter. It's just more gel circulating through the tank.

I *knew* Big Blue Biter was strange. How long had it been out in the open, an imblobster mailbox, trying to chomp on fingers? I feel strangely good knowing I wasn't the only xenogel creature hiding in plain sight.

But I'm not here to contemplate my kinship with a mailbox. I slip out the door, and then through another marked *Xenomorphic Processing Lab*.

This room is much smaller, just one guy in a lab coat standing at a console, eating a green apple. Before him is a little aquarium. But instead of fish and plastic pirates, it contains only water and one little strand of xenogel.

The man turns a knob. Inside, the xenogel strand squirms like it's in pain.

I'm in pain, too. A sharp ache grows in my skull, like something's trying to gouge its way out with a knife.

He turns the knob further. The xenogel squirms, and I swallow a gasp of hurt.

The man in the coat glances up before looking back down at his console.

"Hey, Tami, how's it going?"

"Great," I manage to say. "Just great. How are you? How's your day? What's up, my good friend?"

"Just about to test the xenomorphic processor before the Blast. Because after that, things are going to get pretty hairy. It's a bad idea, if you ask me."

"Yes, it's a terrible idea," I say with a massive amount of certainty, even though I have no idea what he's talking about. "Just out of curiosity, why do you think it's bad?"

He scoffs. "We haven't done enough tests, we've got unplanned xenoforms walking and talking all over town, and we haven't vacuumed more than a few of them. Woll rushed things, and now we're all going to pay the price."

"Those are all good reasons," I agree.

The "unplanned xenoforms" he mentions must be imblobsters.

He clicks a button. In the tank, the xenogel strand shivers like a struck guitar string, so fast it becomes a blur. I feel like I'm becoming a blur, too.

The man takes one last bite of his apple and then dunks it into the tank. The strand moves toward it like a paperclip drawn to a magnet. When they make contact, the strand is gone. So is the apple. In their place is a huge, round hunk of shimmering gold. It sinks, hitting the bottom of the tank with a heavy thunk.

The pain vanishes.

"Aha!" the man says, smiling like he's having a really good day. He types something on his computer.

I make a hasty exit.

One by one, I poke my head into every room I come across. Some are just offices. Some are supply closets. And in one room, I find a giant, evil-looking device.

Resembling a microphone, the machine towers at least fifty feet above me. Lights cast a sinister red glow over warning signs. Stenciled in black paint on the side are the words *GEOSONIC AGITATOR*.

*Geo* means earth.

*Sonic* means sounds.

*Agitator* means something that agitates.

Dozens of workers in orange vests and hardhats scurry around with tablets and wrenches and screwdrivers, too busy to notice me. They're all wearing headphones. A big computer monitor displays a map of Cedar Creek View with all the sinkholes I know about, and a bunch I don't know about, marked in red.

I step to the guardrail and look down. The device is even bigger than I thought, plunging into a raw hole in the earth where it's too dark to see.

I know what this device does.

It's the source of the Hum.

This is the device that's been causing me so much pain. The one that's been making me lose control. The one responsible for all my problems.

I've finally pieced together the Collaboratory's scheme.

The Geosonic Agitator creates the Hum. The Hum sends sound waves deep underground to create sinkholes and cause pain to the xenogel mass. To get away from the pain, the xenogel tries to escape to the surface. Once the xenogel's out in the open, the Collaboratory sends out crews to vacuum it up. But if the Collaboratory is too late, the gel imblobsters anything it touches, like human beings or mailboxes.

The part I don't understand is why. What does the Collaboratory gain from all this?

I look to the ceiling, wondering what I should do. Sabotage the device? Make sure it never hums again?

On the wall, a clock displays big red numbers.

10:00:00

9:59:59

9:59:58

9:59:57 . . .

It's counting down.

♦ ♦ ♦

The clock keeps ticking away seconds. I bet when it hits zero, the workers are going to activate the Geosonic Agitator, and I need to get out of here before I'm reduced to sludge.

I dig my phone out to text an *Abort mission* message to Agnes, but before I can type a single word, someone says, "Tami, what are you doing here?"

I turn around.

It's Woll.

Ugh.

"Did you bring in Jake Wind?"

"No, he wasn't home. Or at school. Or anywhere. I'll go back out and resume the search. I'm leaving now. Okay, bye."

"Don't bother," Woll says, irritated. "After the Blast, he'll be liquefied. The vacuum crews will suck him up with the rest of the loose xenogel in town."

Why would the Collaboratory want to suck me into a vacuum cleaner and pour me into a tank?

I'm so close to figuring it all out. If I just stay cool and remain Tami for a few more minutes, maybe I can get Woll to spill the rest before the counter hits zero. Then, once I have Woll's confession, I can make her give me Growler back and then maybe shift into a sledgehammer and smack a bunch of people, which is what they deserve for devoting their lives to doing weird and creepy things.

"WHO IN THE HECK ARE YOU SUPPOSED TO BE?"

I know that voice.

It's Tami. Her eyes bulge in anger, as if I've just stolen her burrito.

I have an excellent comeback: "Who in the heck are *you* supposed to be?"

Leonard, trailing just behind Tami, has an idea. "Dr. Woll, let me shoot them both. It's the only way to be sure."

"Hey!" Real Tami and I protest.

Woll rubs her temples. "The Blast is in seven minutes and twenty-three seconds, I am scheduled to release the largest amount of xenogel yet, and I've got vacuum crews deployed all over town. This is supposed to be a big, triumphant moment for me. I even have *Big Triumphant Moment* written in my calendar. And now my Big Triumphant Moment is being complicated by two versions of Tami in the same place. Which means one is the real Tami, and the other is an independent xenogel construct. Leonard, figure out which is which and put the duplicate in the tank."

"Doctor Woll, a moment?" A technician with a red-flushed face mumbles something about a malfunctioning surge protector.

Woll yells, "I don't have time for this," so I guess malfunctioning surge protectors are bad news.

I don't have time for this either.

I have to stop the Blast.

And I can't do it alone.

I look up at the ceiling, fifty feet above my head, maybe more.

"Agnes! Now!"

There's a sharp crack. A ceiling tile tumbles down. A rope follows, uncoiling all the way down to the floor.

And then, here comes Agnes.

She slides down the rope and lands with legs wide and one fist on the ground in an absolutely perfect, ten out of ten superhero pose.

"Smoke bombs!" she screams with glee. "Paff, paff!"

It's pretty cool that she provides her own sound effects.

Our backup plan was having Agnes break into the air shafts from the dead mall and crawl around in the ceiling to keep an eye on me in case I needed help. I think she's a little glad I got caught, because she really wanted the opportunity to rappel and toss smoke bombs and totally be Night Kite.

The technicians are running around frantically, but it takes me a moment to realize they're not reacting to us.

Over the blare of a siren, somebody says something about an uncontrolled discharge.

"Turn it off!" Woll screams. "Turn it all off!"

The clock on the wall says there's more than six minutes to go.

Disaster doesn't care what time it is.

# CHAPTER 16

**THERE WAS A HUGE, DANGEROUS** science device and a countdown clock. Heroes always deactivate the huge, dangerous science device before the clock hits zero. Except for this time. "Aw, man," Agnes says, disappointed. I feel bad for her.

The Geosonic Agitator comes to life with a dreadful floor-shaking thrum. Dust and flakes of ceiling plaster snow down on us. As the haze from Agnes's smoke bombs drifts away, fissures zigzag up the wall. Red dots multiply like a rash on the map of Cedar Creek View. That means new sinkholes. Dozens of them.

Big, bellowing pain blooms in my head and chest and belly. I can't hold Tami's form anymore, and without meaning to, I shift into my most comfortable shape: my own. But I do a bad job of it. I'm me from the waist up, but below that, I'm a lumpy, sticky mess, like a melted candle.

Agnes grabs my arm. "Up on your feet, Jake. We've got to get out of here."

"I don't have any feet!"

"Well, grow some and get up!"

"IT'S NOT THAT EASY TO GROW FEET, AGNES."

"You're right; I'm sorry. But you can do this. Think about the way it feels when your toes and soles and heels bear the weight of your body."

"I can't! The Hum . . . it's too much."

"Don't give up. Remember how it feels to have ankles. And knees. And hips. And a butt."

"Don't talk about my butt."

"Concentrate, Jake!"

She's right. Focus. I have to get out of this room, and I need a lower half to do it.

With a long, slow exhalation, I try to loosen. It's like trying to play guitar with rigid hands. You need to flex and stretch them. You need to warm them up. I must be warm grease.

Gradually, I form feet. Then legs. Then my butt and all

my necessary bits and pieces.

"Dearest monkey, what's going on?" Dairy and Gravy rush up to Woll.

"Kids, you have to evacuate. Tami, Leonard, get Mary and Davey as far from here as you can."

"Yes, ma'am," says Leonard, all snappy and military.

People are scrambling and tearing their hair out and saying things like "AAAH" and "GAAAH" and "WAAAH." Agnes makes a time-out with her hands. "What's the deal with you two, anyway?"

"We're her children." Dairy shrugs, as if she has no idea what "deal" Agnes is talking about.

"But are you her real kids, or imblobsters of her kids?"

Woll lets out a long, weary sigh. "They are my children. A few weeks ago I let them visit the lab because it was Take Your Child to Work Day. I told them not to touch anything."

"We touched everything!" Gravy says cheerily.

"Especially goo!" Dairy chimes in. "If there was goo, we touched it!"

"And then the inevitable happened," Woll says. "But they've gotten very good at being goo. They're quite solid." Woll gives them a proud-mom smile. "Now, you two get somewhere safe. And don't touch *anything*."

"Touch all the things!" the twins cry, allowing Tami and Leonard to lead them away.

"Dr. Woll," a technician screams, "we have a new locus of geological instability."

Woll lets out a frustrated groan.

A big new dot blooms on the map. If I'm reading the map correctly, we're about to get a sinkhole right under our feet.

"I have to get to the tank," Woll says. She ducks under wires dangling from the ceiling and charges from the chamber.

"Hey!" Agnes shouts, dashing after her.

"Yeah, hey!" I shout, dashing after Agnes.

The ground does not cooperate with dashing. A great low moan rises from the depths of the Earth, and the floor tiles splinter. Debris rains down from the ceiling. Water spews from broken pipes, and more alarms cry.

Hopping over a puddle of standing water, Woll bulls into the tank room. The tank is still in one piece, but inside, the xenogel swirls with turbulence.

The gel is in distress.

It's in pain.

It's angry.

I know this, because I'm feeling the exact same things. I feel it in my body because of the Hum. And I feel it in my heart, because it makes no sense to hurt living beings.

Woll checks gauges and meters, *tsk*-ing and shaking her head at what they're telling her.

Things are about to get bad.

"Just tell me why," I ask her, nearly begging. "Just tell me what this is all for."

"I think I know," Agnes says. "The Collaboratory can take a bucket of gel and turn it into anything they want. Food. Medicine. Machines. Weapons."

Or apples into gold.

"We could end hunger," Woll says. "We could end poverty. Disease. We could revolutionize the way we live. We could transform the entire planet. Doesn't that sound worth some risk? Worth some inconvenience?"

"Sure," Agnes says, her voice dripping with venom. "It also sounds like a great way to get very, very rich."

Woll doesn't deny it.

I'm still not satisfied with her answers.

"Why me? Why get the twins to lure me here the first time? Why imblobster my dog? What do you need *me* for?"

"Your friend just told you," Woll says, impatient. "Xenogel is valuable. And you're made of xenogel."

Money. Whatever other reasons Woll claims, they did this for money.

The Collaboratory doesn't care about the Fosters, or about Growler. Or about me. To them, I'm just xenogel. I'm just something they can sell.

It builds within me.

The Hum.

The pain.

The fury.

If the twins could imblobster Growler at will, then I bet I can imblobster Woll. Let's see how she likes it.

But is revenge important? Will it solve any problems?

My teeth grow sharp. "Where's Growler?"

"Who's Growler?"

It takes all my concentration to keep my angry fingers from forming knives.

"Growler is my dog. The one your kids imblobstered. Where. Is. She?"

"Your dog is wherever you left her," Woll says, frantically checking control panels. "Or maybe we got around to vacuuming her up. Maybe she's in the tank. But she's not your dog anymore. When the gel contacts another creature, it transforms the molecules of that creature into xenogel molecules."

Agnes grips my arm, holding me back from Woll. "People and dogs are more than just the stuff they're made from," she says. "They have memories. They have personalities. What happens to them?"

"I don't have time to answer your questions," Woll snaps. "In case you haven't noticed, the Geosonic Agitator malfunctioned and I am doing my best to prevent a catastrophe. So if you could please let me concentrate—"

"Answer her question, Woll, or I'll imblobster you right now. Your choice."

I stretch my twitching fingers toward her face.

"Agh! Fine!" Woll screams, flinching back. "Think of the gel as a 3-D printer. The electrochemical patterns involving consciousness and memory are the design software. Those patterns still exist in the gel."

There's a lot going on. Alarms clanging, Collaboratory people rushing around and screaming, ceilings crumbling and water pipes bursting. But I pay close attention to what Woll is saying. If I understand her correctly—

"We can restore the imblobsters to their original form.

Growler, the Fosters, Mr. Brown . . . everyone."

"In theory, yes," Woll says. "Maybe."

Before I can demand that she tell me how to get Growler back, before she can say anymore, the metal skin of the tank groans and cracks. With a great, ringing *KAAAALLL-LANGG*, the tank blows, steel shards whizzing through the air like bullets, smashing craters in the walls. The xenogel erupts in a torrent of goo, and Woll vanishes under a heaving wave of glop.

I shift so fast that I'm not even aware of what I'm doing, forming a sphere with a hard outer shell and encasing Agnes within, like an egg protecting a baby chicken.

The floor caves in, sagging and cracking apart, dropping us down to the abandoned department store below. I bob and bounce on the waves of xenogel like a beach ball, only dimly aware of Agnes screaming. With the force of a runaway truck, the wave splinters the walls of the department store, carrying us out into the parking lot.

The wave continues on, gathering itself into a gelatin mass, at least thirty feet tall, gurgling and pulsating with tons of glass and steel and wood and plaster and creepy mannequins suspended inside. It roars on, rolling away from the mall, swallowing cars and trees and anything else in its path. When it reaches the edge of the parking lot, it starts to lose energy, slowing down and finally coming to a rest.

A moment of tense stillness hangs in the air.

With one magnificent *sploosh*, the sound of a mammoth toilet flushing, the great blob loses shape and sinks back into the ground.

I revert to my Jake shape, spilling Agnes onto the parking lot surface. We lie there, exhausted and panting.

"What happened?" Agnes says, her voice a frog croak. "Is it gone?"

"How should I know?"

And yet . . . I do.

I can feel it.

The blob is part of me. I'm part of the blob.

It's not gone.

It's only fled underground.

And it's on the move.

I think about my dad, driving to school to pick me up.

We need to get back home.

# CHAPTER 17

**HERE ARE SOME OF THE** things Agnes and I witness while pedaling home:

A guy on his hands and knees, munching his front lawn. He smiles at us with grass-stained teeth.

Cupcakes with hummingbird wings flitting about a cactus.

A chicken crossing the road that turns to us and meows with disdain.

A girl on the corner singing, which would be okay if she only had one mouth instead of six. Her harmonies actually sound pretty good.

Agnes and I agree to check out our houses and make sure our parents are okay. Agnes's place is the first on our route. As we lay our bikes on the porch, she pauses at the front door.

"I don't know what I'm going to do if my mom's an imblobster."

"How about run?"

"But what if she gets on the phone and tries to do real estate stuff? What if she sells a house to a dog for two dollars?"

That's not what Agnes is really worried about.

She's already lost her dad. I won't let her lose anyone else.

"Remember when Tool Man replaced Night Kite's butler with a robot that had meat cleavers for arms?" I ask her.

"Issue 17, 'The Cutler.' Night Kite blew its head off."

"Right, but then she found her real butler alive and it was all okay. No matter what, it's going to be okay, Agnes."

"It's going to be okay," she repeats to herself.

Instead of using her key, she picks the door lock, because she's Agnes.

Her face is a tense stone as she slowly pushes open the door. We stand on the doorstep and peer inside.

Her mom is at her desk in the living room corner, talking on the phone. Her computer screen displays a house, and I can see a lot of zeroes in the price. She is not attempting to sell a house for two bucks.

Her mom glares at us. "Why aren't you in school?"

"I was on a mission, Mom."

"Edna, will you please excuse me, I have to attend to something. Yes, yes, I know there are sinkholes all over town, but I'm sure property values will recover. I'll call you back as soon as possible. Thank you."

It doesn't sound like she's talking to a dog. Another good sign.

"What do you mean 'a mission'?" she bellows. "Your 'mission' is to be in school."

"She's normal," Agnes says to me, her face relaxing.

She shuts the door, and we get on our bikes with Agnes's mom screaming "AGNES OAKES, YOU GET BACK HERE THIS INSTANT!" so loud the windows shake.

"Totally normal," Agnes says.

Seeing Agnes's mom being normal gives me hope that not everything in town is imblobstered. But hope fades when we get to my house.

The saguaro cactus in the front yard blinks at us.

Because it has eyes.

Big, blinking green eyes.

We step around it and approach the front door. I crack it open but remain on the porch. Inside, xenogel pools on the carpet. It drips from the ceiling. It runs down the walls.

The TV is on, tuned to the local news.

"All is well," says a smiling newscaster with stiff hair. "There is no news. Eat milk."

Mom cradles a bar of soap as though it's a baby bunny. She kisses it. "Did you know soap is congealed fat? Hello, Jake. Would you like to say hello to your congealed baby brother?"

Oh, no.

They got Mom.

Growler stares blankly at the wall, not growling.

"Is . . . Dad here?"

He steps out of the kitchen. "I am here, baby soap! And I could use your opinion on something. How many butts do you think I need?"

He turns around.

He has four butts.

"AAAAAAUGH," is my response.

These aren't my parents. That's not Growler. They're imblobsters, no different than fake Mr. Brown. No different than the cactus in the front yard that blinks at us as we leap on our bikes and flee down the road. Leaving them behind feels like ripping hair from my scalp, but we ride away as fast as we can.

"Where to?" Agnes says, breathless.

"Dale's Guitar Shed."

"Your cousin? Isn't he already weird? How will you tell if he's an imblobster or not?"

That's a fair question, but Dale is family, and I won't let him face an imblobster invasion alone. Also, he has something I need.

Downtown is even more imblobstered than my neighborhood. A postal worker happily stuffs mail into a storm drain while a Chihuahua leaps from palm tree to palm tree like a flying squirrel. A fire hydrant sprays a gusher of what looks like blood but I really hope is not blood. Parked cars chuckle as we ride past.

My hand hesitates on the door when we get to Dale's. The guitar shop has always been a safe place for me. It's a refuge where I don't have to watch what I say. I don't have to follow rules. I don't have to be careful. I can just play my heart out, and Dale's always been here to listen.

With a deep breath, I lead the way inside.

Things look okay. The weathered carpet is made of

carpet, not fish scales. The guitars on the wall are still guitars, not jellyfish. And, like normal, I have to say Dale's name four times before he looks up from his workbench.

"Dude! Check it out!" he says with a happy grin. He plugs Basszilla into a towering amp and the air buzzes. When he plucks the lowest string, the floor vibrates with an impossibly deep, low note. "Gnarly, right?"

I squeeze my eyes shut against the sound waves. He's still Dale.

Agnes goes straight into interrogation mode. "Have you noticed anything strange? Any unusual customers? Talking animals? Plants with eyes?"

"Nah, you're the first ones through the door today."

I kind of love how Dale takes Agnes's questions in stride. I just hope he does the same with what I'm about to tell him.

My stomach flutters, like I'm standing on the edge of the high diving board at the pool. Here goes nothing.

"Dale, I have something to tell you. I'm an alien made of goo from a long-dead planet and after crossing millions of miles I hard-plopped in the desert where my mom and dad found me and then I assumed human form and now the rest of the alien blob is bubbling up all over town and replacing everything it touches with weird imblobster versions and we don't know what happens to the original people and animals and things it takes over and it already got Growler and Mom and Dad and you should probably try to get out of Cedar Creek View before you get imblobstered." I refill my lungs. "Also, I need to borrow Basszilla."

"Gnarly," Dale says. He holds Basszilla out for me.

"Dale, I just told you I'm an alien goo boy."

"Yeah, I figured it was something like that. I can always see sound waves rippling through you when you play loud. I'm really attuned to vibes. Because I'm a musician."

"But . . . you never said anything."

"I thought I was just seeing things. I see things, you know. What about Agnes? Is she an alien, too?"

"Pfff, I wish," Agnes says.

"Cool. So, you wanna try the bass?"

I love Dale.

The bell hanging from the door jingles and a man enters.

He looks normal, a big guy in a long-sleeved blue shirt tucked neatly into khaki pants. The name tag pinned on his shirt is from the bank across the street. It says *PHIL*. His smile is so unnaturally friendly that I instantly recognize him as an imblobster. Also, he's wearing his shoes on his hands.

"Hello, people of the guitar. I wish to purchase a musical noise screamer."

Agnes and I brace for action, but Dale doesn't get it. "Sure, what kind of music do you like? Electric or acoustic? What's your budget?"

I stare hard at Dale and wiggle my fingers in a way that's supposed to somehow communicate, "IT'S A GOO PERSON!"

But Dale just thinks I'm waving at him. He returns my finger wiggle and goes back to talking to the imblobster.

"Are you an experienced player or are you just starting out?"

"I am just starting out," Goo Phil says. Face noodles shoot out from his cheeks, twitching through the air for Dale.

My arm stretches in a way only possible for another creature made of goo. I crank the volume knob of Dale's amp. "Dale, pluck a note!"

Dale hits the fattest string on his monster bass. The amp emits an explosive rumble that blenderizes my chest. The floor shudders. Dust falls from the ceiling. Pain thunders through my insides.

This is exactly what I hoped would happen. Basszilla can mimic the Hum, at least on a small scale.

"I feel funny," Fake Phil says.

"Do it again!" I wheeze through clenched teeth.

This time Dale hits the string with more precision and more force. I feel myself losing shape, sagging like a rotten pumpkin three months after Halloween. But I will ride out the storm. I will remain Jake-shaped. I *will*.

Fake Phil makes a gargling noise, like his throat is made of Vaseline. He loses form and collapses into a splash of xenogel on the floor.

Dale's feelings are hurt. "Why did you try to attack me like that? I was just trying to sell you a guitar."

The puddle pools and glides across the shop, under the door, and away.

"I'm not sure it was an attack," Agnes says, wearing her thinking face. "Imblobstering is an adaptive behavior, an instinct to take on the form of things in an organism's environment. Like a chameleon changing to the color of its background, only way more sophisticated. Maybe the Blast has Phil feeling freaked out and vulnerable."

It makes sense, kind of. "But why don't I have that instinct? Even when I was a baby blob right after I splash-landed, I didn't imblobster my dad. I just took on human form."

"Maybe because you weren't freaking out," Dale suggests. "Your mom and dad are nice people, so if the first thing you saw when you arrived on Earth was someone loving you, then maybe love is a vibration. The love vibe keeps you from wanting to grab people with your face."

"We are not calling it the love vibe."

Agnes frowns like she's working on a complicated math problem. "That would even explain Dairy and Gravy. They don't go around imblobstering everyone they meet or touch because they have a mother who loves them. Or at least a mom who keeps them safe so they don't feel threatened and freaked out all the time. I think Dale is right! The love vibe is the key!"

"We are not calling it the love vibe!"

Agnes gives me a stubborn look. She is totally going to keep on calling it the love vibe.

I can only sigh. "You and Dale have to get out of here

before the gel turns you two into cauliflower with bat wings."

Agnes says "ha ha" without laughing. "Obviously I'm not going anywhere without you. So what's the scheme, Jake?"

"I'm going to take Basszilla and blast every imblobster to jelly."

Dale winces. "That sounds . . . mean."

"I don't know what else to do, guys! The blob took Mom and Dad. If I don't do something, there'll be nothing left in Cedar Creek View that isn't an imblobster. And from there the blob will expand. It'll take Carefree and Gila Bend. It'll take Phoenix and the Superstition Mountains. It'll take all of Arizona. It could take over the entire world. I have to stop it."

"Music isn't supposed to hurt people," Dale says. "I never would have taught you guitar if I thought you were going to use it as a weapon. Music is supposed to be about communicating. About expressing thoughts and feelings there aren't even words for."

"Dale—"

"No, wait," Agnes says. "I have an idea. What if . . ." She pauses, working out details in her head. "What if instead of using Basszilla to blast the gel, you used it to play the love vibe."

"*We are not calling it that.*"

Excited, Agnes starts walking around the shop. "Dale, do you have a tone phaser and a frequency modulator?"

Dale points to a display case of guitar effects pedals. "I have several. What kind of music do you like? And what's your budget?"

I ignore him and turn to Agnes. "You think you can adjust Basszilla so instead of simulating the Blast it emits . . ."

"Say it, Jake."

I grit my teeth. "The love vibe?"

"Yes. But we can't do it here in town. The gel is too scattered. And we need a bigger sound system."

I know where to find one.

I can't help but grin.

I'm going to live my dream.

I'm going to play Desert Sky Pavilion.

# CHAPTER 18

**THE SINKING SUN PAINTS THE** sky with desert purples and pinks and oranges glittering with the first evening stars. There's no concert scheduled at Desert Sky Pavilion tonight. Rows of empty seats spread out before us. Beyond them stretches a lawn where people sit on blankets or dance during shows. But right now it's just an empty amphitheater.

The venue will be full soon enough, and my first-ever public performance will have to be spectacular.

Dale wanders the stage in a bit of a Dale haze while I unload our gear: Basszilla, a big bass amplifier, effects pedals, and Stringy, which Dale insisted I take along in case I need my best horse. Whatever that means.

I roll the amp up on stage while Agnes emerges from a storage room with armfuls of coiled cables. She plops them on the stage floor in front of Dale. "Okay, Dale, your turn. Plug us into the sound system."

Dale just stares into open space. "Dude."

"Dude," Agnes says. "Plug us into the sound system."

Dale licks his dry lips. The drive out from town was a bit much for him. "There was a lady whose entire head was just one big strawberry. She was trying to eat ice cream. There were monkeys with chainsaw hands. Or were they chainsaws with monkey bodies? And you want to bring them here?"

I guess it's one thing to learn the cousin you've been giving guitar lessons to is an alien made of goo, but monkeys with chainsaw hands might have been too much for poor Dale. He sits on the stage. "I need to breathe. Dude."

Agnes sighs and picks up a cable. It's up to her. "This is like *Night Kite* issue 103 when she had to assemble a proton beam cannon to stop a tsunami from wiping out Grimm City."

"How did I miss that one? Does she save Grimm City?"

"I don't know, it just came out last week and it ends on a cliffhanger."

"Obviously she's going to succeed."

"*Night Kite* sales aren't doing great, and she might get canceled."

"Oh."

Agnes looks at her phone. "'How to Set Up a Concert Venue Sound System.' Let's see. Digital signal processor, impedance levels, direct input box, XLR cables . . . Okay, I think I can do this." She starts plugging things into complicated-looking wall sockets and connects the tone phaser and the frequency modulator and the Hum-o-Tron in a daisy chain of cables to the amp.

She throws some switches. Huge speakers overhead hum to life. Basszilla vibrates in my hands.

I place a finger over the lowest string and pluck as hard as I can. My kneecaps vibrate and soften.

"Are you okay? I have a cold compress."

"I'm okay," I grunt."

Simulating the Hum with Basszilla is painful but necessary. We have to prove that we can make a big, awful noise that affects xenogel. But the goal isn't to hurt the imblobsters. We need to change the sound so it attracts xenogel like a bug light draws flies.

Agnes turns some knobs. "Hit it again."

I strike another note. It's even louder and bigger, and my body buzzes violently, as if my blood is made of bees.

For all I know, my blood *is* made of bees.

But with some more adjustments, the notes I play start to hurt less, and I feel less like cake batter in a mixer.

I give Agnes a thumbs-up.

"Okay, pied piper, keep playing. With any luck, we'll be swarmed with imblobsters before long."

"How is that luck?" Dale moans. "The monkeys had chainsaws."

I keep playing, nothing in particular, just scales and rhythms, just making noise. But I'm sending out a signal, like a whistle only dogs can hear. In this case, it's a vibration only xenogel can feel.

"Try not to rush those eighth notes, dude." Even while freaking out, Dale still manages to coach me.

Something moves in the dark behind the fence at the back of the amphitheater. A shadow, gathering, accumulating, growing. It writhes and jiggles, a gelatinous wall of half-formed imblobsters and raw xenogel. Giant turtles and insect-motorcycles and flying cupcakes and the monkeys with the chainsaw hands and dogs with human faces and a shark on tank treads and palm trees slithering on their bellies like snakes and hundreds of other imblobsters.

We did it. We brought the blob here.

That was the easy part.

We attracted the blob but that doesn't mean I can control it. Maybe instead of drawing it out of town, I only made it mad. I have to reach it somehow. Get it to stop making more imblobsters. See if I can communicate with those electrical-chemical patterns Woll told us about, the memories and personalities—the essence—of the people and creatures the blob took over.

The imblobster blob spills over the back seats, merging together in a wave of arms and legs and wings and wheels. It's louder than the speakers, louder than Dale's endless refrain of "Dudes, I am freaking out."

I gather my thoughts and take a deep breath, fingers poised over the strings. I can do this. I can find the right notes, the right frequency, the right language to tame the blob. This can work.

It has to.

Now or never.

The moment of truth.

I fret a note and pluck a string.

A wisp of bitter smoke poots from the amp. Basszilla

makes a sad little *fffzzz* and then falls silent.

"What just happened?"

Agnes frowns. "I think Basszilla fried the amplifier."

Ugh.

The imblobster wave keeps coming.

Agnes's eyes flicker back and forth. She's thinking so hard I can almost smell her brain cooking. "Giant bass fiddle cricket!" she says. "Please tell me you looked at *Physiology of Animal Species, A Zoological Compendium* and got to the chapter on fiddle crickets."

Only a few weeks ago if someone yelled "Giant bass fiddle cricket" at me, I would have had no idea what they meant by that.

But now I've been through some situations. I've seen things. I've *been* things. I've read *Physiology of Animal Species, A Zoological Compendium.*

I've been a seal. I've hidden a tablet in my belly. I've been Tami. I've protected Agnes inside an egg.

So I close my eyes.

Take a breath.

Be less clenched.

Be less congealed.

I can do this.

My legs shift into triple-jointed limbs, thick as tree trunks. My arms stretch into forelegs. Extra legs emerge from my sides. My soft human belly separates into armored segments while my skin hardens to shell-like armor. Holes down my sides draw in air, replacing my need for lungs. My two human eyes shift into a pair of simple eyes that turn the world from color into just light and darkness, and I grow another set of eyes that lets me see in every direction at the same time. My head changes shape into something resembling a hard nut with antennae more than half the length of the rest of my body. Most importantly, I grow four wings.

And I am enormous. My head nearly reaches the catwalks above the stage. Below, Agnes and Dale are little dark splotches, and if I'm not careful, I could crush them.

All I have to do now is rub my hind wings together. Just the slightest brushing already produces the deepest, loudest sound I've ever heard. It's like an orchestra of cellos if the cellos were the size of cruise ships. I could grow more wings. I could grow bigger wings. I could create noise that would make Basszilla sound like a ukulele.

The xenogel mass keeps coming, thrashing, out of

control. It wants to get to me. It wants to get to Agnes and Dale. I can sense its desire to imblobster the world. I can sense it because I'm part of it. And it's already cost me so much. Xenogel took Growler and Mom and Dad. Xenogel cost me my friendship with Eirryk. It's responsible for me being #MallSeal.

What made me think I could reason with it? What made me think I could control it? And why should I even try? All I have to do is rub my wings and blast the xenogel. I'll be like Star Hammer in double-sized issue 50, "Family Matter," when the last survivors of his home planet, the remaining Bahlpeenians who happen to be evil, come to take over Earth. Star Hammer uses the Celestial Mallet to destroy them, and that's how he becomes the very last Bahlpeenian in the entire universe.

That's how I'm going to deal with the xenogel.

I will blast it to mist.

I will reduce it to molecules.

To atoms.

To subatomic particles I don't even know the names of.

That's how I'm going to deal with this weird, conglomerate alien creature.

This weird alien creature . . . that I'm part of.

But this isn't how the people in my life who matter—my mom and dad, Dale, Agnes—would treat me. Mom and Dad knew I was made of alien goo from the very beginning. Agnes stayed my friend even after I told her what I am. Dale has always accepted me. And he's even weirder than I am.

I don't need to be a gargantuan cricket right now.

I need to be something else.

I close all my eyes again. I suck air deeply through my side holes. I imagine the pointy bits on the ends of my legs playing guitar delicately, with control.

Uncongealing, I shift back into my Jake form.

Agnes runs up to me. "What happened? Re-form the cricket!"

The blob mob advances.

"No time to explain. Just give me Stringy."

Agnes doesn't question me. She hands me my old guitar.

I give it a strum. It's out of tune, but that doesn't even matter.

My fingers pick some slow patterns in a minor key. The sound is cold and dark and lonely. It's like leaving behind a home you can never return to. It's dreading what's ahead.

The blob keeps coming, huge, towering.

Next, I play a fast run of descending notes, plummeting from the sky. With a windmill swing of my arm, I hit a power chord. Even without amplification, it sounds massive and violent, the music of a falling object smashing to Earth.

Then I grow extra fingers. I make chords that would be impossible with human hands. My song doesn't sound like any other music I've ever heard. It's chaotic, confusing, out of rhythm.

It's alien.

It's not knowing where you come from, who you are, what you're supposed to do, what you're supposed to be.

I play the song of me to the blob.

And the blob sings back.

The blob calls me *segment*, a word that means something closer than brother or sister, closer than friend. It's a word that means the blob and I are just different parts of the same being. When it sings to me, it's like I'm singing to myself. Our song is about how we left our world when our sun exploded. How we broke up into thousands of globules, spreading across the galaxy, looking for a new place to call home.

Our bit sailed through the endless winter of space, across distances that would require a dozen zeroes to express with a number. We huddled together in a congealed ball of xenogel for thousands of years, until we splashed to Earth in the desert of Arizona, on the edge of this human habitation of Cedar Creek View.

The impact broke us apart. We were no longer one. We were scattered bloblets, droplets, a disorganized mist, and we soaked into the ground, exhausted and frightened.

Except for the segment that is me.

Because I was found by people who loved me.

I became human.

Twelve years later, the Collaboratory's sound-making weapon attacked us. We were dealt pain, and we were confused, and we were used.

"Just tell me what you need," I play on my guitar.

"We need . . ." the blob plays back in a deep, thrumming melody.

"Yes?"

"We need . . . *you*."

"Why? For what? I want to help you."

"We need you . . . to help us . . . go home."

"Okay! I will do that! Just tell me how!"

"You must . . . complete . . ."

"Complete what?"

"Complete . . ."

"Please complete a sentence."

"You must complete our spaceship."

We play more at each other, and when we get to the end of our song, I know what to do.


The blob hovers above us, a towering wave ready to come down and crush everything.

Agnes peppers me with questions.

"What did you sing to them? Did they say anything back to you? Are they going to stop attacking? Can we get everyone to normal?"

In answer, the blob starts to plop and bubble like boiling pudding. It spits out parking meters and trees and mannequins. It spits out birds and cats. It spits out a postal worker. A chef. The guy from the bank across the street from Dale's Guitar Shed. One by one, it gives up the objects and creatures and people it's absorbed. It spits out dozens of strangers, but also Parker Zeballos. Mr. Brown stands in a daze, goo dripping from his hair and limbs. It spits out a bewildered and be-gooed Eirryk. It spits out Collaboratory workers. It spits out an angry Dr. Woll.

Finally, it spits out someone I am desperate to see. She growls in as much fury and outrage as a nine-pound dog can muster. We run to each other, and still growling like this is all my fault, Growler leaps into my arms.

And then, after several minutes of nervous watching, somewhere around the twentieth row of the amphitheater, among hundreds of dazed and confused people and normal chairs and parking meters and motorcycles, I spot my mom and dad standing knee-deep in xenogel.

I run to into their sopping, gooey hugs. They're freaking out.

"I'm fine. What do you remember?"

"We were both working at home. Your mom came up with a new soap slogan—"

"Soap gives hope," Mom says, still disoriented but proud of her new emotional soap slogan.

"A sinkhole formed in the backyard," Dad continues. "And there must have been some kind of leak. There was gooey stuff everywhere."

"Gooey stuff. Did it remind you of anything?"

Mom nods thoughtfully. "Oh, yes, we came out with a new shampoo a few years ago, but it didn't take off. We called it Shampooze. Customers complained it was too oozey."

"Dad?"

Dad rescues me. "The goo was like you, Jake. The way you were when we found you. Only bigger, and so much more of it."

"It's the same stuff that I'm made of, Dad. In a way, it is me. We're part of the same blob that splashed on Earth twelve years ago."

"Keep it down, Jake," Mom whispers, alarmed. "People will overhear."

In the past, I might have been angry and annoyed at Mom and Dad trying to restrict what I say, where I go, what I reveal about myself. And I am annoyed. But I also love them for it because they love me, and they're trying to protect me in the only way they know how.

"Don't worry," I say, with kindness. "My secret's about to be blasted wide open."

Dad puts a hand on my shoulder. "I don't know what's going on, but we need to get you out of here. Let's go home."

Gently, I shake off his grip. "There's something I have to do."

"Jake, what did you promise the blob?" It's Agnes. I don't want to tell her what I promised, because I know she'll try to talk me out of it, and I'm afraid I'll let her.

"I promised to leave Earth with them."

# CHAPTER 19

**"WHAT DO YOU MEAN YOU'RE** leaving Earth?" Dad demands.

"Pretty much what it sounds like, Dad. The blob wants to go to space."

Mom puts her hands on her hips. "Jake Wind, under no circumstances are you to fly into space."

A ship traveling to other stars must be able to survive millions or billions of miles across empty space. It has to withstand extreme temperatures and radiation and airless wastes. A spaceship like that is the most complicated kind of machine imaginable, and the blob needs to have all its parts to form such a thing.

It needs to be whole. And that means it needs me.

The blob wave broadens and flattens, forming something like a colossal manta ray hanging over the seats and blocking out the moon. It spreads its wings, graceful and mighty and beautiful.

Xenogel globules lift off from Mom's and Dad's hair and from bits spilled on the ground and from flecks stuck to all the cats and dogs and creatures and people that were part of the blob. The globules rise through the air to join with the ever-expanding manta ray.

I feel myself drawn to the ray as well.

"Can I come with you?" Agnes asks.

"No," I tell her with regret.

"Are you going to come back?"

"Yes."

"Promise me."

"I promise I'll try as hard as I can. You have goo in your eyes."

"Those are tears, you dope. And you have them too."

"Will somebody please tell me what's happening?" Mom says. "I don't understand any of this."

"I'll fill them in," Agnes says. "You go do what you have to do. Oh, hey, there goes Dr. Woll."

Woll is trying to sneak over the fence at the back of the amphitheater.

I wipe my tears and give Agnes a Night Kite salute. "Go get her."

Agnes wipes her tears and returns the salute before charging off in pursuit.

Mom and Dad won't let go of me, but I can't let them hold me back any longer.

I inhale and relax my muscles and shift into pure liquid. My body stretches into a long goo strand, rising high, reaching for the manta ray. My parents' cries of "Jake, come back!" and "Jake, don't do this!" and "Jake, you are so grounded!" cut through the muffled gasps and "ooohs" and "aaahs" from the crowd.

When I make contact with the ray, it soaks me up like a sponge. There's no longer me and the blob. We are one thing. We want one thing.

Our segment landed on Earth. Perhaps other segments from our world landed on other planets. We will find our other segments and rejoin them, becoming an even greater One.

We rise like a hot air balloon. Below, the people of

Cedar Creek View look like an audience milling around after a big show. I wonder if anyone recorded my song. I hope I played well.

We're so high up now that the lights of Phoenix are a glowing yellow circuit board. Above, the stars shine clear and twinkle-free. The planet is a broad curve, frosted with clouds.

We have a lot of work to do before we reach the top of the atmosphere, higher than birds and bugs can fly, where there's no air to breathe and the temperature is cold enough to freeze blood.

Our gel shifts into an impenetrable outer layer, thin as an eggshell. We form a whole separate brain capable of navigating between stars. We form cells that generate energetic impulses to power us through space.

The blob couldn't do this without me, and I definitely couldn't do this without the blob.

I remember how much strength I get from knowing my parents accept me, and from knowing Agnes accepts me. In their eyes, I'm not a weird kid. I'm me, and it's good and okay to be me.

Being part of the blob is that feeling times a hundred thousand.

And now we are a spaceship.

Our engines gather power, vibrating through every atom of our massive body.

"We're ready," we tell ourselves.

It's funny to think that just a couple of weeks ago, I was afraid of growing a bird hand in public. Now I'm the most powerful machine on Earth. In the entire solar system. Maybe in a dozen solar systems.

I remember how Agnes encouraged me to shift. She was never afraid of me or what I could do. She never thought I was weird.

No, that's not quite right.

She *does* think I'm weird, but my weirdness doesn't bother her. She likes me *because* I'm weird.

And that's why it's easier to do this: to go where I belong.

Which is home.

My real home.

Because the blob is me and I am the blob, it knows what I'm about to do.

"We are enough now, segment. Thanks to you, we are all that we need to be."

"Are you sure?" we ask ourself.

"Are we ever sure of anything? It is not in our nature to be sure. We do what we must anyway, even when confused and uncertain."

The spaceship is built. It won't be complete with me gone, just as I won't be complete without the rest of me. But we will be enough.

"Good-bye, then," we say to ourselves. "We love us."

Peeling myself away from the blob hurts. It hurts my heart, even though I don't have a heart right now. It feels like ripping off my own head and leaving my body behind.

The spaceship, the thing I was for just a few moments of my life, streaks off into the dark.

Without a motor, I fall.

I reenter the atmosphere, flames licking the edges of my goo puddle. The ground rushes up at me.

I hope the space blob finds more of us out there.

If not, I hope it finds friends, wherever it sets down.

And I have one more hope as well.

I hope it doesn't hurt too much when I pancake in the desert.

# CHAPTER 20

**WITH STRINGY IN MY HANDS** and Growler curled up in my lap, I sit cross-legged on the roof and look out over the humble lights of the neighborhood.

There are still no cedar trees and no creek or view of either in Cedar Creek View. It's a weird place. It's a town that has seen shapeshifting goo. It's a town where at least half the residents were imblobstered.

Some pretend it never happened.

Some say there was something in the drinking water that messed with their minds.

Some know that Dr. Woll and the Collaboratory are behind everything.

Woll should have gone to prison after Agnes caught

her trying to flee Desert Sky Pavilion and turned her over to the police. But it turns out the Collaboratory's parent company, uniMIND, can afford a lot of lawyers. Woll and the Collaboratory may never have to take responsibility for their role in shifting the town against its will. In some ways, that's the weirdest thing of all.

My phone buzzes. It's a text from Agnes.

"EMERGENCY: GHOSTS AT THE DEAD MALL. WE MUST INVESTIGATE."

"Ghosts?" I text back. "Seems unlikely."

"Agreed. It's probably mannequin imblobsters that didn't rejoin the blob. Whatever. We gotta look into it."

"It's a school night. How about Saturday morning?"

"I think now would be better."

"You're already at the mall, aren't you?"

"Yeah, but don't worry about it. I'll be fine. It's just a bunch of mannequins with CHAINSAWS."

"I'll be right over."

At the beginning of this story, I wouldn't have been able to tell you who I am, even with thousands of words.

Let me try now.

I'm Jake Wind.

I'm twelve years old, and I'm a Cedar Creek View Middle School student.

I'm an alien from a planet that hasn't existed for thousands of years.

I am made of xenogel.

I'm the son of two constantly worried and freaked-out parents.

I'm a guitarist.

Sometimes I'm a seal.

I'm a friend of Agnes Oakes.

I am all these things, and as my life goes on, I'll probably change a lot and be a bunch of other things, too, just like anyone else.

Right now, I'm a boy with a long squid arm that I use to deposit my very growly dog back in my room.

And immediately after that, I'm a screech owl, taking flight from my roof and soaring on warm updrafts above turquoise backyard swimming pools.

I'm a person, which means I'm too complicated to sum up in even a million words.

But I can do it in one.

I'm me.

# ACKNOWLEDGMENTS

My name is on the cover, but without the work and help of a lot of people, there would be no book. It would just be my name, floating in space. Which would be weird. So, I would like to thank those who made everything less weird.

At HarperCollins, thanks to:

Erica Sussman, my patient editor, whose judgment and sense made this book so much better.

Tom Clohosy Cole for his beautiful, eerie, and evocative cover illustration.

Chris Kwon and Alison Kapthor, whose design skills turned a wonderful cover into a wonderful-looking book.

Deanna Hoak and Jessica Berg for catching errors,

deviation from typographical norms, missing words, and inconsistencies.

Louisa Currigan and Stephanie Guerdan for the editorial work that helped turn my story into a book.

Nellie Kurtzman, Robby Imfeld, and Audrey Diestelkamp for their unfairly invisible but absolutely crucial work marketing this book.

Mitch Thorpe, publicist, without whom so many fewer people would know this book even exists.

At Root Literary, thanks to:

Holly Root for guidance, reassurance, commiseration, and laser-eyed focus on my interests.

Melanie Castillo and Alyssa Moore for boosting my work and all the dozens of tasks that help a writer sleep securely at night, knowing things are being taken care of.

At the water cooler, thanks to:

Jenn Reese and Sarah Prineas for helping me with earlier drafts of this book and listening to my incessant whining.

Hans Haas of Wavelength Brewing Company in Vista, California, for telling me how concert venue sound systems work. If I got it wrong, it's not his fault.

At home, thanks to:

Lisa Will, my best friend, partner in all things, wife, and all-around awesome human being.

Dozer, fuzzy beast creature.

Amelia, other fuzzy beast creature, whose personality is depicted in the character of Growler.